INFLUENCE

Book One of the Influence Series

By David R. Bernstein

DAVID R. BERNSTEIN

Bernstein, David R.
Influence

10 9 8 7 6 5 4 3 2 1

CONTENTS

1
FOOLISH EMPATHY

I CAN'T SENSE his awareness. He could be dead, but even the deceased emit a faint echo that my mind normally picks up. The way he's propped up against the old, rusty signpost with his head dangling to the side makes me think he's been there a while. It's not like I make it a point to hang around corpses, so maybe it's just that conscious imprints fade with enough time. I really don't know.

Amanda couldn't care less as she yanks on my arm, forcing me back to the road. A pit in my stomach tightens my breathing as my typically cautious approach to strangers fades a bit. Amanda always focuses on keeping my ability a secret over everything else, but her concern isn't reaching me.

"I don't know about this, Kay," she says as I drag her small frame back toward him. "This isn't our problem and we can't stop now. We need to get to Bullhead before it gets dark."

She knows traveling in this desert wasteland at night adds another layer of danger to our situation. There's something about the darkness that brings out the worst in desperate people.

"I know, I know, but what if he's alive and I'm just having an off day or something?" I bite my lower lip as I think of what to do next. "The guilt of leaving someone to die is going to hang over our heads."

Staring beyond the cracked and crumbling highway, I track a tumbleweed moving through the lifeless expanse. Even it is taunting me to move on. Ignoring my doubts, I lean in and check for a pulse. Amanda groans while she rolls her eyes in disapproval. My fingers swipe across the stubble of his neck as I search for signs of life. "Oh crap…" I bite down harder, "…he is definitely alive."

"That's not possible," Amanda says, knowing my unique skill has never failed to give us a heads up before. "Now what?"

"Grab his legs," I say without hesitation.

"I swear… Times like this, you really show your age."

I can't stand it when she says that. It's not like being seventeen is that young, considering how messed up the world has become. She means well and her heart is in the right place, but just because she's older than me doesn't mean I can't think for myself.

We drag his lean but heavy body off the road. Patches of taller brush will provide some much-needed shade from the intense late afternoon sun.

I might not be the bravest person, but I'm also not one to pass by someone in need. I've been an orphan since I was three—I know what it feels like to have no one in the world who gives a crap whether you live or die.

Amanda found me six years ago, and all that changed. She's five years older than me, from the once-resource-rich sector group known as the Terrance Party. They were a group of former renowned political families who, toward the end of society, came together in hopes of creating a new government for the former United States.

Drops fall from the young man's forehead as I use some of our precious water supply to cool his exposed skin. I can feel Amanda's eyes burning a hole in the back of my head, and I know she doesn't approve. The guy, who doesn't look much older than me, begins to breathe more comfortably. He looks peaceful as we trickle fluids into his mouth, which force him to swallow. His dried and cracked lips peel apart as he sips in small amounts of oxygen. Each exhale expands and is deeper than the one before. The immediate threat to his health appears to have eased, but our next step is still unknown.

"We have to go now," Amanda urges, looking at the fading horizon. "It's going to be dark in an hour or so.

We don't know who this is and I really don't care. Let's go."

"Let me think a minute, okay?"

It's been almost eight hours of pushing ourselves way too hard to reach this town. There's nothing but dust, heat, and more dust between Bullhead and our last supply stop. Even before we stumbled upon this guy, the water bladders we each carry on our backs were nearly empty, and we still have an hour or two to travel. Sweat trickles off my ponytail and down the back of my tank.   The stinging heat is dragging us down. We wouldn't normally attempt this long a trip, but the chance to stock up on food rations is far too tempting to pass up. Waiting here much longer will only lower our odds of reaching Bullhead before nightfall. With the limited resources in the Lost Souls sector, there is really no choice but to take these kinds of risks. Lost Souls is one of the last sectors that is not controlled by corrupt groups. Not that there's much to control here anyway.

"Let's at least wake him so he can try to move on before it gets too late," I say.

The unknowns involved in this idea really test my dedication to empathy. That plus, for some strange reason, unlike every other person I meet, I'm unable to feel this boy's consciousness. This fun fact makes me reevaluate.

"Are you crazy?!" Amanda shouts, eyes wide. She looks almost frantic as her body tenses. I've never felt this from her before.

"Okay, okay, fine. But, wondering if we left him to die is going to haunt me," I say while Amanda tugs on my arm, leading me away.

"Wondering is better than *us* dying, Kay."

We're edging closer to the road when we hear a raspy and desperate voice call out to us.

"Wait, please don't go." His voice struggles to carry the ten yards or so we've walked.

We turn to find him staggering to his feet, legs wobbly. Without a second thought, I run and put my shoulder under his arm and try to support his solid frame. Amanda rolls her eyes again, but she still manages to find the compassion to come and support the other half of his body.

"Thank you." The words barely escape his mouth.

I look up at him and give a cautious smile. Dark hair covers his eyes as he continues to regain his strength. His breathing looks more natural now and he starts to carry more of his own weight. As he pulls his head and shoulders up, his stature is more noticeable. He is much taller than me, and I am not short.

My long legs make traveling easier than it is for Amanda. Having to work for everything in this expansive sector doesn't allow for us to be lazy. Each town or outpost is miles and miles apart. You rarely see working vehicles anymore and when you do, they often come from a neighboring sector group's scout patrol. Constantly traveling by foot forces us to remain fit and strong.

I catch myself as I scan his body, noticing his clothes. They are not the common, tattered apparel of the people from the Lost Souls sector. Uncertainty fills my mind, but I guard my reactions and act casual. His pace slows, and his head turns back to the road sign where we found him.

"Can you guys hold on a minute?" he says, slowly walking back on his own. "I forgot my bag and supplies. I hope it's okay that I tag along for a bit."

With his back to us now, my eyes lock with Amanda's as I mouth the word *"clothes."* She nods in understanding. The outfit he's wearing had to come from an outside sector group. The last remaining shops were ransacked long ago, leaving little for choice in Lost Souls. You never see people with new, complete outfits unless you are part of a sector group's organization. Unlike our mismatched clothes, his look is put together with a purpose. The stiff, buttoned-up, dark navy shirt and matching cargo pants can't make traversing this sector pleasant. Our suspicions are confirmed as we get a good look at what we recognize as a Magnus-issued backpack he returns with. Brown and plain with only one subtle yet distinctive marking. If we weren't so familiar with this logo, it would be easy to overlook: embroidered, red double lines that trail the side of the pack. The lines are supposed to represent all paths leading to the Order. Amanda and I again exchange glances; we both know we need to act cool.

The Magnus Order spreads across most of the former state of California. Their ruthless expansion is well known in Lost Souls. The Southern Coastal region is the sector bordering ours and Magnus mostly controls it.

It was a neighboring sector group like this guy's that overran Amanda's Terrance Party. Nothing remained of her childhood home. Her parents died defending her group's ideals. Amanda was lucky to make it out before they placed her for assignment against her will.

"Thanks for waiting," he says as he combs his hair back with his free hand. The gesture allows us to finally see his full face. No longer hidden by his shaggy, dark brown hair, I can't help but notice the strong facial features. His sculpted jaw line and solemn brows draw you into his eyes. It looks like he's due for a haircut, but the style suits him.

He rummages through his bag as he calmly says, "My name is Farren, by the way. Farren Knox."

I swallow as my heart races. He digs deeper into the backpack. Does he have a weapon? *He can't know what I am.* Amanda's face whitens with fear; she must have come to the same conclusion.

We jump back as Farren pulls something out. His brow tightens, noticing our reaction.

"Take it easy, ladies, it's just a snack," he says while the side of his mouth inches up in apparent amusement.

Three hydro-nutrition bars crinkle in his hand as he zips up his pack.

"Sorry, we don't know you, and your sector clothes scream *stranger-danger*," Amanda blurts out.

"I am just passing through," he insists while handing us a bar. "I'm on my way back home, that's all. I was visiting family here and pushed myself too hard. Luckily, you found me."

"Hey, Amanda, we don't have time for this." I try to change the subject.

"So, *her* name is Amanda, and you are?" His eyes narrow and his head tilts to the side as he focuses on me.

I pull my ponytail over my shoulder, combing through the damp ends with my fingertips. Scanning over the sealed package, I wonder if it might be laced with something. What have I gotten us into?

"Where is home?" I ask, ignoring his question. "Oh, and thanks for the hydro-bar."

Apparently Amanda wasn't worried about getting drugged, as she has devoured half of her bar. Glancing at her, she shrugs as if I'm crazy to be cautious about eating it. We pick up our pace and continue walking north as the sun sets on the western horizon. No longer able to ignore my rumbling stomach, I dig into the moist, lime-flavored treat. I forgot how good these were. The snack gives us energy and has a slight hydrating effect, thus the name. Farren is able to keep pace with us as his dehydration continues to wear off.

"I live with the Magnus Order." He pauses, as if reconsidering his words. "I know what you're thinking—

that I must be evil or something, but hear me out. I was forced to work for them."

"How were you forced to work for them?" Amanda asks, knowing full well how manipulative sector groups are.

He takes our wrappers and stuffs them in his pack before returning his attention to Amanda.

"If I didn't, they would take it out on my family. It's that simple."

"What kind of work do you do that is so important they need to threaten your family?" I ask, knowing that the Magnus Order has no honest work to offer.

"Well, I am a..." He looks straight ahead, avoiding our eyes. "I am what they call a Push Recruiter."

My heart drops into my stomach as the reality of what Farren says sinks in. There is no need to ask him to explain, we know exactly what he is and what he does. The man we saved represents everything Amanda and I are running from. The recruiters scout out the neighboring regions in search of promising Influencers, like me, who they can take back to their group for placement, most often against their will. Regardless, those *recruits'* lives are changed forever. Manipulated by whatever means necessary, they are forced to spread the influence of the group, expanding its power in the region and beyond. Strategically placed like beacons, Influencers help shape the reality of the nearby population. The people 'pushed' are then steered to the desired outcome, which is usually to be submissive and stay in line with the group's interests.

How can I be this stupid? We've been so careful for all these years, but now I am side by side with the enemy. If I use my push ability on him, it will only expose me and make me a target for every recruiter they have.

Not wanting to tip him off about what I am, Amanda follows my lead and we play along for now. I inform him of our destination and we all decide to stick together until we reach Bullhead. From there, Farren will continue on to the Magnus sector. With him not fully recovered, he needs us. Traveling at night just became a little safer with this guy around, as well. If we can pull this off, that is. With no working infrastructure for electricity, the lack of lighting will make it very dark very soon.

2

INFLUENCER

A PUSH RECRUITER and an Influencer traveling together is not uncommon these days, but normally the Influencer is manipulated or being forced. The fact that I'm choosing to do this is terrifying—and dumb, but our only option.

It's been more than six years since I've been this close to someone discovering my abilities. The last time, I almost killed two people.

It was a couple of years after Amanda and I met at the ironically named Hopeful Outlook Shelter in the Lost Souls. I was eleven and she was sixteen at that time. That was our last stop before we started our lives as wandering, homeless kids.

Hopeless, as the kids call the shelter, gives the impression that they are a place where orphaned children find refuge and begin a new life, but we all know they just operate to find recruiting opportunities for nearby sector groups. There's no effort made to actually find homes for the children. Having a family requires finding more food, and dragging the kids around puts you at greater risk of being discovered by the ever-present sector personnel who troll this area. That means few are interested in taking in extra mouths to feed unless there is a strong blood tie.

It's not only Influencers who catch the eye of these recruiters. Having any valuable skillset makes you a prized target. Living in an Influencer-guided sector strips you of your freedoms, and the worst part is you are completely unaware of the manipulation.

While living at the shelter, I discovered something strange and quite frightening. The way I perceived and interacted with the world had changed and I was no longer a naive young girl. One day stood out more than any other in my life, and the events of this day changed everything.

It was like a switch was flipped. My life of being normal in a less-than-normal world ceased to exist. This event will be burning in my head until the day I die. Something awoke inside of me and I had no clue what it was until it was too late.

I can still smell the burnt chemical odor of the cafeteria. The walls dull and free of personality. Functionality and purpose are all that matter to the sector sponsors. The end goal is not to help children, but rather to help themselves. The emotional wellbeing of the child is secondary to the discovery of untapped talent.

Amanda and I entered the mess hall for what would be the last time. The eating area consisted of several long, folding tables and an assortment of mismatched chairs all lining a poorly ventilated room that had once acted as a storage wing. After the staff handed out our prepackaged meals, we found a couple of spots on the rusted and wobbly table toward the end of the room. No one usually sat at that table since one bump would topple it over, but Amanda wasn't big on making friends. Distance from the rest of the kids was perfect.

We forced down bland rations and expired cans of fruit as we kept to ourselves. It started out as any ordinary day, but that would not last.

Alex and Billy Wilson approached our table, arms folded, flexing their unnecessarily large muscles. Their eyes trained solely on Amanda. The Wilson brothers were troublemakers and not the kind who played pranks on people—rather, the kind who lived to create chaos, pain, and fear in others. The boys' attitudes had led four shelters to expel them before they invaded ours.

With devious grins, Alex, fifteen, and Billy, seventeen, headed straight for Amanda. Billy had been in several fights in his short stay at this shelter and looked ready for one more. You could not overlook Alex, well over six feet tall and I guessed close to two hundred pounds. He made for a dangerous and rather intimidating sidekick to Billy.

"Hey, Snob," Billy hissed. "I heard you came from the Terrance Party. It must suck to be here with no maid to serve you."

"I bet you think you're better than everyone here, right?" said Alex.

The boys inched closer to us.

"Well, you know what?" Billy said, leaning in. "You guys didn't put up much of a fight when we took over your homeland. Our Southern Alliance made quick work of your fancy little party group."

The Southern Alliance was a sector group that controlled most of the southern region of the former United States. The group didn't like the idea of "political elites of the past," as they called them, forcing their way of life on their people. The rigid alliance saw it necessary to take out Amanda's Terrance Party.

"When we took over your homes and ended your new government fantasy," Alex said, "you guys stood there helpless, holding on to your stupid books and fancy clothes while your town burned."

Amanda's jaw locked, grinding her teeth, then she lashed out at the brothers. "Your *alliance* is nothing more than a bunch of hicks with pitchforks who are afraid of the outside world," she said. "Besides, it looks like they didn't care too much for you two idiots since your parents threw you out like the rotten food the shelter dumps out for the dogs."

Blood brightened the brothers' faces. With one swipe of his hand, Billy knocked over our table. It crashed against the wall, quickly drawing the attention of the other kids in the room. Amanda and I scuttled back to the cool cement wall at the rear of the mess hall and huddled together.

With spit flying out of their mouths, the brothers snarled as they edged closer, cornering us. The hatred that clouded the air was something I had never felt before. Amanda placed an arm across my midsection in a futile attempt to protect me. These boys could've snapped our necks in seconds.

Alex grabbed Amanda by the shoulders and lifted her off the ground. Amanda was a head shorter than him, and easily outweighed by a hundred pounds. Her body scraped against the rough surface of the backing. Failing to find a concerned face in the crowd, I wondered why none of the shelter staff had stepped in. Then I remembered who sponsored the shelter: the Southern Alliance. Amanda had been struggling with the recent sponsorship change for the last few weeks. One trait those people were known for above all else was their unyielding loyalty to anyone associated with their sector group. At that moment, I knew we were alone and hope was fading fast.

Amanda's legs hung about two feet off the ground as Alex pushed her higher up the wall. Fear and anger grew as I watched my only friend in excruciating pain.

"Stop, leave her alone!" I shouted. Not even a quick glance made it my way. I was as insignificant as the ants on the floor.

My fingernails dug deep into my thighs. I looked into the faces of the kids in the mess hall and prayed someone would step in to protect us. Their faces ranged from scared to excited to indifferent. I was a rat trapped in a corner. My heart felt like it was going to rip out of my chest as I searched for help. None came.

Seconds later, I felt an inner shift and my mind focused as it never had before. Surrounding sounds became softer and diluted. Details sharpened and reality narrowed into a funnel before my eyes. The entire room became an accessible focal point. I heard the kids' jumbled thoughts racing around my head. The chaos would not last. It wasn't long before their disjointed inner dialogue was sucked out of my head and our minds became unified and quiet. Captivated by what was going on, I connected with the onlookers in the room. We were one mind, one stream of thought. An incredible sense of unity and clarity filled the mess hall. No longer did I feel like an individual. I had a lock on their minds. I could see it in their eyes; their attention had completely shifted to the brothers.

Slipping out of the heightened state, I turned my attention to Amanda. With her fragile body pinned high up on the wall in Alex's fierce grip, Billy continued to hurl disgusting slurs at her. Doubt about my so-called mental powers entered my thoughts when a jarring, loud *whack* echoed off the wall. A metal serving tray fell to the ground, narrowly missing Billy's head. The brothers snapped out of their intense lock on Amanda only to turn and find at least twenty motivated youth ready to attack. Alex dropped Amanda as the brothers faced the unexpected, angry mob.

"What are you fools looking at?" Billy said.

Amanda sat still as she caught her breath, then turned to find me. She retreated to where I sat crouched up against a trash can near the rear wall. Then, with little warning, the shelter kids attacked.

Serving trays and utensils acted like weapons as the boys and girls lunged at the brothers. Forks and knives sliced the brothers' limbs; trays pelted them from all sides. Only the cries and screams of the boys could be heard. No longer did they sound like the hulking figures who had been about to hurt Amanda. Brought to their knees, battered and bloody, the crowd overran the brothers. Only when the threat ended did the mob snap out of their rage.

They staggered out of the mess hall as though not sure what had happened. Toppled over on the filthy floor, the brothers were swollen and almost unrecognizable. I watched them barely breathing and became horrified at what I apparently caused. Amanda, still in a state of adrenaline-filled panic, grabbed my arm and forced me out of the mess hall, then out of the shelter completely.

After what felt like miles, she finally ran out of steam. We found ourselves at an abandoned restaurant where we stopped to regroup. We made our way into the broken-down kitchen and collapsed against a metal workstation. After several minutes of catching our breath, Amanda turned to me.

"It was you, wasn't it?"

"Yes," I said without thinking. "I don't know what to say—it just happened, I guess. One minute I'm watching you about to be killed and the next I'm creating some sort of mental link with the kids in the room. It happened so fast. It was horrible."

Amanda's former Terrance Party had been taken down with the help of what she called *Influencers*. Never having any experience with this crazy phenomenon, I never really understood what she was talking about. I just knew she resented them and partially blamed them for the loss of her parents.

Amanda's hatred for Influencers made it hard for me to look into her eyes. Was I really one of them? Would she hate me now as well?

Instead, Amanda took my hand in hers. "Thank you, Kaylin. Thank you."

Right then, I knew things between us would be okay. Amanda has always been able to make me feel like everything would be all right.

"We can't ever go back there, or to any shelter again," Amanda continued. "They're aware of you for sure and I know word of the powerful push you did will bring in recruiters from all the nearby sectors."

"Push? What do you mean?"

"From what I've witnessed, no one has ever had a push happen that quickly and never that directly. It always takes time and outside planning for the push to force change. I've never heard of anyone able to change the focus of a group of people so quickly and with such direct intention. Those kids just freaked out on Alex and Billy."

"I know, it was awful." I sighed.

"We can't talk about this with others. They will take you and make you do horrible things," she insisted. "Those evil sector groups are crawling all over this area."

Filled with uncertainty, my mind shifted to what had just happened. No matter how horrible they were, I always had empathy for life in whatever form it came. I melted into Amanda's arms and cried for what would be the last time in years. Life had changed. I had changed.

I was now an Influencer.

3

PUSHED INTO A CORNER

I WAVE MY hand up at the crimson-tinted horizon in hopes of manipulating the setting of the sun. *Please stay up for a little longer.* The excessive heat has given way to a more bearable temperature; still hot, but bearable. Right now I would take the baking sun over the perceived dangers that hide in the night. But, this is not the only worry Amanda and I face as we are one slip-up from putting ourselves squarely in the sights of the self-serving Magnus Order. Running from Farren is not an option. If we travel with him, we increase our chances of making it safely to the town of Bullhead. Our only choice is to continue to play it cool, for now.

Farren has recovered fairly well in the short twenty minutes of traveling we have done together. The water and hydro-bars have given him the strength to maintain the faster pace Amanda and I have set. Even knowing what he is and where he comes from, I'm still glad we did not leave him to die.

"You never told me your name," Farren says as he trails a step or two behind me.

"I'm Kaylin," I say as Amanda shoots me more disapproving looks.

Farren notices her continual disdain and edges closer to both of us as he matches our pace.

"You know, you guys can trust me." He puts a hand on both of our shoulders. "I'm from Lost Souls like you. I grew up here."

"Well, life has taken you on a different path, hasn't it, *Magnus Man*," Amanda says as she shrugs her shoulder away from Farren's hand.

His hand still remains on my shoulder. Even though it makes me uneasy, his touch doesn't feel like the grip of a ruthless hunter. It's gentle, somehow kind.

"Wouldn't you do anything you could to protect your family?" he asks. "You don't know anything about me, Amanda."

She edges closer to Farren and says, "It was sector groups like yours who destroyed my home and killed my family. Why should we trust you?"

"I'm sorry about that, but my job has nothing to do with either of you." His hand leaves my shoulder. "I have a job to do. If I don't do it, they will come into Lost Souls and hurt my family. Again, it's that simple."

"Look, it's getting dark and we have to stay together if we want to make it to Bullhead, so let's put all that behind us," I say while shooting Amanda one of my own looks.

Several minutes pass with no one saying a word. Only the setting sun reflecting on a few wispy clouds on the horizon remains. Luckily for us, the moon gives off some faint and cool light that helps guide our steps as we travel. My mind jumps from what I've gotten us into, to how our chances of making it to Bullhead become worse with every passing minute.

The silence is broken as I stumble on a rock, letting out an awkward screech.

"Stupid darkness!" I shout while blood flushes my cheeks. Luckily, this same darkness hides my embarrassment from sight.

Farren offers me a hand. "Are you alright, Kaylin?"

I don't accept his help, pushing myself off the ground on my own.

"Thanks, I'm fine." I force out a smile.

Once we're moving again, my curiosity gets the best of me. Though I know I should not be making an effort to learn more, I can't help myself.

"So, Farren…" I tug at my ponytail to tighten the band, "have you recruited anyone against their will?"

His head jerks up. "That is not who I am," he says. "I find people who are looking for something new and have the certain ability Magnus wants. I don't hide what I do."

"A certain ability, huh?" I will probably regret what I say next. "You mean Influencers who get used to manipulate people?"

He stiffens and his mouth cracks open in surprise. I don't think he was expecting me to know so much about Influencers. Amanda steps in to cover my careless mistake.

"If it wasn't for those recruited Influencers I would still have my home and family," Amanda says, the words laced with venom.

"Not everyone has been negatively affected by Magnus," he says. "Some people are simply starving and want a more stable life. One of the few good things about these sector groups is they do provide for their citizens and to some, ignorance is bliss. I'm not saying that's right, but desperation makes people do things."

To me, there is nothing a sector group can provide other than corruption, control, and fear. Why anyone would be willing to fall into the manipulative fold of one of these groups is beyond me.

"Ignorance is not bliss when your family is killed by these evil groups," Amanda says, walking a few steps ahead.

"Why don't you just pretend to not find anyone when you go out on your recruiting missions?" I suggest. "You could pretend to be bad at it."

"I wish it was that simple, but they forced me to join them for a reason." He adjusts his pack. "I was trained by my father to be a tracker since the age of seven. Our family became well known in the area because of our abundance of wild game. The Magnus Order has a way of finding people with desirable skillsets."

He opens one of the metallic buttons on his shirt. It shimmers in the moonlight as his fingers free it from its proper position. "Two years ago, just shy of my sixteenth birthday, they forced me to join them. Because of my *talents,* they set benchmarks for my so-called hunting. If I go too long without bringing in some new recruits, they will take it out on my family."

The nearly full moon overhead is all the light that now remains. The only sounds we hear are our footsteps and heavy breathing as we push on through. We estimate we have less than an hour to go before we see the dim lights from the town of Bullhead. The temperature has dropped quite a bit and we are able to move faster now.

"So what is your story, Kaylin? Do you have family close?"

"Amanda is all I have," I say while watching her kick rocks several yards in front of us.

"Can I ask what happened to your family?"

I can see in his face that he is genuinely interested. His eyes have a way of gently squinting when he concentrates on me. It's like he's trying to fix a problem that he doesn't fully understand.

"There really isn't much to tell," I say, shrugging. "I was told that someone dropped me off at a shelter door when I was three years old."

I exclude the part about the necklace that I had wrapped around my waist at the time. Only Amanda and my initial shelter caregiver know about this. And Lilly, who took care of me for a little over a year but died before I turned five. It's the only piece of whatever past there was that I have. I have kept it tucked under my shirt for safekeeping since I was four years old. Even though gold is worthless today, the pendant is unique enough to kill for. The fine strand of interlocking chain has held up over the years. I never understood what the design of the pendant is supposed to represent, if anything at all. It has three linked pieces with bars that spread out from three points in a circular pattern. It's beautiful, and I hold out hope that I might one day understand its significance.

"Being in shelters your whole life must have been hard. I am sorry," he says.

Opening up to him is not the smartest thing I could do, but it takes my mind off whoever might be lurking out there. Amanda and I have heard bad things about this stretch of road at night.

"So you don't know anything about your family? No last name, nothing?"

"Nope, and with how the world is, who really needs a last name?"

"Well, I am glad you at least have Amanda in your life, even if she does hate me," he says.

I look ahead and realize this conversation has slowed our pace. Amanda is quite a bit ahead of us now.

"She is not usually this rough around the edges," I say.

The three of us push on with the moon overhead and our packs empty of food and water. We need to get to this town and need to get there now. Our bellies are grumbling and our mouths are dry. Amanda has been quiet for some time now; that's usually because she's hungry, but with Farren around I don't know for sure. Or maybe she is finally tired of giving me those looks that say a thousand words.

We're scanning the horizon for any sign that we are getting close to Bullhead when a dim light far up the road grabs our attention.

"Finally," Amanda shouts up ahead. "The sweet lights of a town full of food!"

Farren grabs my shoulder and stops. "Hold on," he says as his eyes study the horizon.

The dim lights flicker, and don't resemble the steady glow of a town in the distance.

"Why are you two stopping?" Amanda says while eagerly waving us on. "Let's move and get our reward!"

"Be quiet, Amanda," Farren says in a subtle voice. "Those are not the lights of Bullhead."

I look at the concern on his face and quickly turn to Amanda and notice her jogging ahead of us.

"Harvesters," he says as he grips my shoulder and pulls me back a few steps. "We need to hide, now!"

I've never actually encountered so-called Harvesters before, but these merciless thugs are the reason we need to get to Bullhead before nightfall. My mind races as fear spirals through my thoughts. We have put ourselves right in the path of the most ruthless delinquents that roam the darkened roads of Lost Souls. They earned the name simply because these people scavenge at night looking for resources to *harvest* from the foolish who travel after the sun has set. It looks like we're the fools tonight.

"Wait... Amanda!" I yell as Farren guides me off the road and into the cover of the brush.

Amanda races ahead before she realizes what's on the horizon. Now, I watch as she comes to a dead stop, paralyzed. She looks back toward the spot where Farren and I had been just seconds before, and I can see her confusion when she realizes we're gone.

Farren has led us to an overgrown patch of dead brush several yards off the road. I can't take my eyes off Amanda, still frozen in the middle of the road. The Harvesters are getting closer—I can hear the sound of an electric vehicle humming toward her. I try to mentally push her to find cover, but I can't break through her panic.

A rusty, dented pickup comes up over the hill. It stops a few feet past Amanda. A gust of wind from the vehicle tosses her long hair over her face. She jolts back into motion.

It's too late, though. I get up to save her as four men jump from the truck and approach her. Farren grabs my arm and jerks me back to the ground.

"No," he mouths to me, shaking his head. His eyes convey his urgency, but it's the grip he has on my forearm that keeps me rooted to this spot.

"Well, this is a fun treat," a voice echoes from the dim-lit road. "Are you lost, little lady?"

Amanda freezes in place as the hulking sounds of heavy feet stomp her way. Out of the crowd, one man, who looks like he is wearing a sleeveless fur coat, shines a flashlight on Amanda's frightened face. His tattered cowboy hat covers his eyes as he tilts his head at her like a curious dog. Dirty, stringy hair dangles out from his hat like greasy strands of yarn as he inches closer to her. Amanda's eyes scan the ground for some sort of weapon.

"Eyes on me," he says. "I asked you a question."

"Umm... I..." Amanda struggles to find the words. "My crew is on their way to pick me up right now."

Amanda's lie has little effect on the men. Their faces change, and they resemble nothing so much as a pack of wild dogs that have cornered their prey. One man, shirtless and slender, rubs his hands together as he nods his head in excitement. The rest circle her, inching closer. I rise to one knee and dig my fingers into the dirt. I have to help her. *Do something, Kaylin. Do something.*

"You see, this is my stretch of road and you have not gotten permission to pass through," he says.

There is a twang to his voice that you don't hear anymore. People don't stay in one place long enough to develop accents; this man is nothing but a stain on the region that hasn't been removed.

"So what we're going to do here is take an inventory of what you have to offer us as payment for your lack of judgment," he snarls.

As one, the men look Amanda up and down. My chest tightens as the four men creep closer to her. Quickly, Farren digs through his bag and grabs something as he gestures for me to stay put. He gets up to a crouching position and vanishes into the dark cover of the brush as he moves closer to Amanda and the men.

Only a second or two pass before I hear a heavy clank and a bursting sound that rattles the brush in front of me. All four men duck and frantically look around trying to see where the blast came from. Farren emerges from the cover of the brush pointing what looks like a Magnus security pistol at the men. I recognize the high-tech look of the weapon that only official sector group personnel carry. Even in the dark, these weapons stand out. The darkened metal and shielded handgrip are dead giveaways. Once again, I wonder what we got ourselves into by rescuing Farren. I don't sense he's a threat to us, but he is still part of the Magnus Order.

"Get away from her, now," Farren urges as he shifts his gun sight from man to man. "I will kill all of you."

"Is this sweet little thang your prize, young man?" the leader asks, his head down and his hands in the air.

"I am no one's prize," Amanda shouts, and she kicks the leader squarely in the back with the sole of her boot.

Sweat flies from his hair as he falls to the ground. He struggles to regain his breath as he gets back up.

In a shallow voice, the man whispers, "Well, that wasn't very sweet of you, was it?"

I get up to go to Amanda's side. I'm almost there when a fifth man emerges from the shadows, moving too fast for me to warn Farren. The man comes up on Farren's blind side and smacks down on the arm that holds the gun. The weapon breaks free from Farren's grip and scrapes across the road, sliding to a stop under the Harvesters' truck. I run at the assailant, hoping to catch him off guard, but one of the other Harvesters spots me and with a vicious backswing of his heavy arm, I'm driven back several feet to the ground. Three of the men overtake Farren and start pounding on him from all sides while the fourth man restrains Amanda. She looks at me and gives a simple nod. I know exactly what she's thinking. The determination in her eyes says it all.

Clearing my mind, I do not hesitate. I focus on the collective consciousness of the Harvesters. The onward approach of the man who knocked me to the ground appears to slow as my mind alters the movement of time for our collective reality. The clarity of the moment sharpens the visual details. Surrounding sounds fade out and at once the slow-witted thoughts of the men cloud my mind: lust, rage, despair. It's a disgusting feeling to be connected to these men.

Shortly after, I sense my own being expand out of my body and engulf the immediate area. A warm haze blankets our surrounding reality, sealing those involved. The overwhelming presence of the Harvesters becomes silent and I now push thoughts of mistrust and hatred at the men. Scattered sparks of light flicker before my vision as entangled energy fuses consciousness. Reality is altered and I sense a shift in the men as my push has changed the mood of the incident.

The charging Harvester abruptly stops after a few steps and looks at me with his grimy face and soulless eyes. He looks as if he has conflicting thoughts running rampant in his head. His eyes shift from side to side as he tries to put them together. A few moments later the push takes hold as he squints and quickly shakes his head, jarring his confusion loose. A ravenous snarl overtakes his face as he changes direction toward his fellow Harvesters. The seeds of mistrust I planted in him have bloomed and his existing vile nature amplifies the intensity of his aggression. Fists clenched and head down, he rushes at the pile of men who continue to attack Farren. His chest and shoulders rise and fall as a wolf would before it pounces on its prey. He grabs the Harvester leader by the neck and thrusts him off the pile.

"Darius," he growls the leader's name, "you've brought me down for the last time. I'm going to end you right now!"

Darius crawls back a few feet as his fellow Harvester pulls out a small hunting knife and closes in.

The shirtless man who restrains Amanda pushes her aside. He assesses the scene before racing toward the truck, intent only on getting away. Amanda crawls to a large rock and lifts it as she gets to her feet. Without hesitation, she smashes it over the head of one of the men who is fighting with Farren. The staggered Harvester falls to the ground face first. Blood trickles down the crown of his head, forming a small pool that reflects the light from the moon. Farren has only one attacker left to deal with. He regains control of the fight as he pins the Harvester to the ground, a knee on his throat. Amanda and I run to each other and embrace. We turn our attention to help Farren when the fleeing Harvester returns with Farren's gun. He points it in the direction of Farren. A second later, a loud *bang* shakes the ground, and the fight is over. Farren scuttles back several feet, but to his surprise, it is the Harvester he was fighting who lies dead with a gaping hole in his head.

The blast from the weapon distracts Darius's attacker, and Darius lunges on the confused man. Within seconds, the leader has disabled his fellow Harvester and redirected the knife into the side of the man. He falls to the ground holding his critical gash. Darius then grabs ahold of his neck, twisting life from the man in one horrifying motion. A kinked body falls limp to the paved road; now the only Harvesters that remain are Darius and the man with Farren's gun.

"I knew I couldn't trust you, Eddy," Darius barks to the armed man as he twirls the hunting blade in one hand. "You've been after for me for years."

Amanda, Farren, and I cautiously regroup on the side of the road. I hold Amanda as Farren stands in front of us.

Eddy points the gun at Darius. "How could I be worried of something so weak? Looking at all of you fools reminds me how you've been holding me back for far too long."

Darius moves quickly and flings the knife at Eddy, piercing his chest. He falls to his knees. He then charges Eddy only to be knocked back by the blast of the gun as it puts a hole in his belly. Darius collapses on himself as the life leaves his body. Shallow breaths are all that Eddy has to hold onto as the blade has punctured one of his lungs. He struggles to breathe as he spits out mouthfuls of blood, eventually losing the race as he chokes one last time before toppling over.

I stare at the horror that lies before me, my heart heavy. Although not by my hand, I have killed five men and I will have to deal with the weight that will tug on my soul.

Farren wastes no time and takes charge by ushering us to the newly abandoned Harvester truck.

Shaken by what has unfolded before our eyes, Amanda turns to me and asks, "Are you okay?"

Words fail to escape as shock locks my body.

We see Farren go back to collect our things; he pauses to evaluate what just happened. *Does he know?* He signals that he's going to get his pack in the brush and he disappears in the dark.

Breaking from the shock, my mind jumps back and forth with thoughts of taking the truck and leaving him, but he risked his life to protect us from those men. We can't do that to him now.

It has been several minutes since Farren left to find his pack in the brush. I'm worried and call out for him, but there is no answer. I tell Amanda I am going to go look for him, but she stops me and volunteers to go instead.

"You have done enough, Kay," she says. "I'm sure he just can't find his pack. I will go help him."

Amanda has apparently changed her attitude toward Farren. His willingness to step in and save us has softened her protective exterior. She jumps out of the truck and quickly fades into the black landscape.

"Farren, you lost?" Amanda calls out in the distance.

Several minutes pass before I see the brush begin to shuffle. Deep panic overruns her voice now as she screams for me instead. Quickly her calls stop and the uncertainty of what lies out there begins to enter my body. I worry that more Harvesters might be out there, but that does not stop me from going after Amanda. Leaping out of the truck, I rush toward the roadside only to be brought to an uneasy stop. Farren's solid frame lumbers toward me with Amanda draped over one of his shoulders and the Magnus weapon in his free hand pointing right at me. Shock sends ripples of energy down my back. *How could I have failed to read this imposter?* My instincts about people are never wrong or, at least, that is what I thought. I feel naive and foolish.

"I am sorry, Kaylin, I have no choice," he says while shaking his head. "I am beyond overdue to bring someone in and the threats to take action on my family have intensified."

He looks disgusted by his actions, but I will not let him suck me into his lies again.

Hoping my push can be played off I plead, "What are you talking about; what have you done?"

"I have never seen anyone with the abilities that you have; the precision, the power. It was remarkable," he says as he sees right through my act. "I can't go back without something. I just can't."

"I saved your life." I struggle to find the right words. "How could you do this to us? What have you done to Amanda?"

He looks at her and stumbles to say, "No-no-no, she isn't hurt. I have only sedated her."

"I am not going to let you get away with this," I say as my eyes well up with emotion. "You will suffer for playing us."

I calm my nerves and begin to push my influence out toward Farren. Thoughts and feelings of panic enter the surrounding conscious fold. My mind reaches out to entangle his helpless consciousness. I will make him flee into the dark desert until his legs give out and his heart stops. The push reaches Farren, but I do not hear his thoughts, I don't sense the connection happening; something is wrong. I take a step back to gather myself and find Farren inching closer. He looks at me and I sense that he knew it would not work. My faulty ability around him goes beyond not being able to sense his awareness. It's useless on him.

"It is called a Push Block implant," he says while carefully resting Amanda in the bed of the truck. "Most official sector group personnel have them implanted now."

"Of course, why wouldn't these paranoid groups have a mad scientist on hand," I say while rolling my eyes in frustration.

"I don't know where it came from, but most of the sector groups in the region have implemented this precaution," he says. "It has something to do with disrupting the magnetic field around the brain."

With a subtle gesture, he asks for my hands. With a gun pointed at my head and lacking any special gifts, I reach out my arms in compliance. He confines them with some sort of plastic wrap that forces my hands together as unusable fists. Guided to the Harvester truck, I sit next to Amanda as Farren loads our packs and other salvaged supplies from the area. I manage to brush Amanda's soft, blonde hair from her face with my forearm before a quick, sharp pressure pricks my arm. I look back to see Farren with a syringe in his hand and an ashamed look on his face.

"I am sorry, I can't have you unleash the world on me as we travel, just keeping us all safe."

Warmth radiates from my arm and spreads throughout my body. I'm at ease for the first time in a long while. The cool bed of the truck counters the heat flowing from the effects of the sedative as I lay back. My eyes flutter and roll upward as the once-protective light from the moon slowly evaporates, leaving me lost in my own mind.

4

BELLY OF THE BEAST

STRETCHING UP, MY hand is completely encompassed in what feels like the grasp of a giant, though the grip is soft and warm. Someone is guiding me, but all I can see is a distorted cloud around the face of an immensely tall being. My eyes are constantly forced back down, almost as if I'm not allowed to see this person. Looking forward, I see two blurred forms in front of us. One much larger than the other. My heart races with excitement as a smile fills my face. I realize what's going on. This is not a giant holding my hand, it's my mother and we're walking toward my family. I am just a child, barely conscious of the world around me. Warmth takes over my body and I try hard to clear the haze that surrounds the faces of the people who obviously mean so much to me. Muffled voices call out my name. They sound familiar as I release the hand of my mother and eagerly run to them. I edge close to the tallest figure when suddenly I hear a deep thud and we are thrust several feet into the air. Before we have a chance to land, the beings evaporate into a smoky haze. The surrounding backdrop begins to brighten as if an immense sun is burning holes in the setting. Flickering light forces me to squint as I try to open my eyes. Tall evergreen trees tower over me as the now normal-sized sun glimmers through the openings between the branches. I'm jolted up again as the familiar hum of the electric Harvester truck thrashes about on the uneven dirt road. My shoulder is throbbing from pounding into the side of the vehicle.

My experience was nothing more than a sedative-induced fantasy, or it could have been real memories trying to surface. Either way, I am brought right back to the bleak, yet dazed reality of being transported to the Magnus Order against my will.

My eyes struggle to stay open as the sedative keeps me in a loopy trance. In between stages of dozing off and uneasy panic, I start to recognize the area we are traveling through. We're in the foothills of the Sierra Mountains in the Southern Coastal region. The smell of fresh pine that floods into the bed of the truck and those lush trees that line the sloping terrain are a dead giveaway. The height of the sun in the sky tells me it must be late morning. Farren must've stopped in the middle of the night to rest.

I shift my elbow in search of Amanda and nudge her side, but she doesn't respond. She is still out, but at least we are together. I try to stay alert as we continue through the forest, but I can no longer prevent my eyes from rolling back as I drift off again.

***

Thrust awake by the sudden stop of the truck, my head barely avoids smashing the rusty sidewall. The sedative's still working, though; I'm only able to turn my head to see that Amanda is no longer next to me. At the sight, I should be more worried—but I can't summon the will to care. My heart maintains the even rhythm of someone in deep sleep.

Farren tells someone that he just came from the settlement wing. Calm as can be, he tells the man he was ordered to deliver me to the Proprietor of Hawthorne.

"Yes, sir," an official-sounding voice says in response to Farren's words. We must be at a checkpoint of some kind.

I remember hearing of this settlement wing at Hawthorne before. It acts as a sorting station for new recruits of the Magnus Order, and Hawthorne is the name of the southernmost hub for this corrupt sector group. The Magnus Order consists of a network of massive cement structures that were commissioned by several prominent figures toward the end of society. Around thirty years ago, these hubs were built as survival bunkers for the elite who feared the wrath of the world their greed had created. The abuse of Influencers backfired and these powerful people lost control of their corporate empires. The scientific discovery of youth who could affect the collective consciousness of others was supposed to be an enlightening breakthrough, but power has always been more important in this world. The former United States imploded from excessive greed and the financial way of life stopped working. The country fell into chaos and shattered, leaving these titans of destruction to flee to their protective shelters at the foothills of the Sierra mountain range. These structures have since lost their original purpose and have become beacons for this power-hungry group. This web of Magnus strongholds is the last place on earth I want to be.

We have arrived at the main entrance of the Hawthorne hub. I pretend to be fully sedated as two men move me from the truck and load me onto a smaller cargo carrier. My feet dangle off the end of the little utility vehicle. The men place a strap across my chest and snaps click on each side of my secured arms. A soiled towel that smells of mildew keeps my head from resting on the rough, metal surface.

As I'm dragged deeper into the hub, I try one more time to push my will onto the people nearby. My focus feels aimless and I fail to gain control of my ability; I remain paralyzed.

The motorized cart transports me away from Farren, and I wonder what's going on in his mind. I don't need to see his face to know he must be conflicted, as he should be. The only thing that comes to my thoughts when I think of Farren is *backstabber*.

I sneak a quick glance at the Hawthorne hub while we move on; its cracked and weathered exterior is enormous. It rises at least five stories, but lacks any windows. It resembles a modern castle with protruding towers on all four corners manned by security personnel on guard. We already went through one cement wall that surrounded the structure and settlement wing. Keeping one eye open, we inch closer to the main gate of Hawthorne. Metal and thick, this entrance is intimidating.

The prominence of the Magnus Order in this sector is vast. Twenty or thirty of these hubs act like small towns that house its citizens. Each hub is 'tamed' by an Influencer that not only maintains order but pushes out the reach of the group as a whole. It would appear a life of altering the will of people is to become my fate as well.

Brought through the large doors, we cross a short, dark hallway into what I can only describe as a gigantic inner courtyard. This part of the hub looks like a town's marketplace, with merchants and citizens going about their daily routines. If it weren't for the armed guards and the Influencers monitoring the citizens, you would almost think this is a good life for people. Surrounding this area are towering walls lined with multiple levels of what look like small living quarters that stretch up to a dark metal roof that covers the hub. I'm nearly caught while scanning the area, as one of the security personnel sitting up front turns to check on me. He just misses my wandering gaze. I need to be more careful. If I could just get my body and mind to fully work again, I would have no problem creating chaos with all these people shuffling around. I remember Farren telling me that only the Magnus personnel have the block implants. Then all I would need to do is slip out the side through one of the numerous hallways.

The air is stale and cool as we move deeper into the hub. The towering walls that shelter this little village block the fresh pine from the surrounding evergreens. Sounds from the courtyard fade and my legs shake in nervous anticipation. I tighten my muscles, hoping to conceal my growing panic. My heart races with such aggression that I fear the pounding will burst out of my chest. *Stupid heartbeat—just shut up already.* We stop as one of the men pushes an intercom to ask for access. This must be where the so-called proprietor of the hub operates. I overheard Farren talking about it before I was dumped off like simple supplies. They sound more like evil overlords if you ask me.

I hear a shrill male voice instruct the men to sit me in a chair at the other end of the room. I don't dare open my eyes to look around, as I can feel everyone is focused on me now. My body slumps in the chair. This is no act. My limbs lack the ability to hold up my body due to the sedative. I can move my left arm a little and I feel some prickliness in my legs, but other than that, I'm lifeless. I hear the hollow sounds of fancy shoes clop closer to me. A heavy smell of flowers and chemicals fill my every breath as someone wearing way too much cologne leans over me. This person clears his throat and swallows as I feel him examining my state.

"Hello, my dear, can you hear me? It is okay to open your eyes now," says a man with a higher-pitched voice. "We are not going to harm you."

Boney fingers grab my shoulder and gently shake me. There is no way out of this now, so I decide to open my eyes and confront my fate.

"Well, there you are," he says with a slimy grin. "Look at those pretty blue eyes."

I remain quiet while studying him and my surroundings. Two men stand guard at the entry to this sterile-looking office. The man who addresses me has his hands behind his back now, leaning uncomfortably close to me. The walls are a dull gray with hanging metallic sculptures that I assume must be art. This is supposed to signify importance and status, but to me, it all just looks cold and lifeless. He wears a tight, fancy gray suit with a bright green tie. The color is so intense that I almost need to squint. He notices as I lick my dry lips and signals the guards to bring me water. His eyes never leave mine as he intently studies my every move.

"My name is Mavis Edgeley and I am the Proprietor of the fine Hawthorne hub," he says with gleeful pride. "We are excited to have you join our Magnus family."

My stomach drops at the thought of joining with this vile group. Knowing Magnus will do whatever it takes to get me to cooperate only intensifies my desire to escape. I try to gather my focus and reach out to anyone who can help, but my push ability fails yet again. I'm powerless.

"Ah, young Kaylin, your ability will not work on me nor my staff," he says as if he saw me try. "We are all protected due to our block implants, but you already know about this, don't you?"

"I am never going to join Magnus," I say, leaning toward his smug face. "You're just going to have to kill me."

He backs up. "Oh, we are not ones to waste talent. You are a smart girl; I am not going to drag this out any longer."

With a large hunting knife, one of the guards frees me from my restraints. He avoids eye contact. I think he's afraid of me. I am handed a bottle of water and some food rations from the other guard. With my one working arm, I guzzle the water down, never taking my eyes off Mavis. He hovers over me while I devour the rations in just a few bites. His face lacks the imperfections the rest of us carry. His flawless, pale skin is just odd. I'm sure he's never seen a day of hard work in his life. It's like he is toying with me as he stands there watching me finish my snack. I get the sense I will not like what comes next.

He grabs a small control device from his large wood desk and turns on two displays mounted in the corners of this office. The crystal-clear screens burst with color as they instantly flicker on. Quickly I recognize Amanda sitting in a room with several other people. He's showing me the settlement wing. I watch this for a few minutes, as I am unable to take my eyes off her sitting near the front desk. Her legs stretch out and her shoulders are slumped forward like a child waiting to be punished by the shelter warden. She is alone and it's my fault.

One by one, the representative in the room calls people forward to her metal desk. Each of them receives a black band and some papers. They're being placed for assignment in the Magnus network of hubs. I'm getting sick of watching. I don't understand why they're showing me this.

The silence is broken as Mavis says, "You see, Kaylin, we like to assign people to places where their lives will have meaning, where they can add to the greater Magnus family."

I realize where this is going and hope I am wrong. I stiffen in my seat as I regain some feeling in my midsection.

"Amanda is quite the caretaker, as you might have already known. We would love to assign her to educate and nurture children here at Hawthorne, but we may find it necessary to place her in the hard-labor division instead."

I can only imagine what she would be put through working twelve hours a day in what is more commonly known as the *slave labor* division. Knowing so much about this sector group should have been enough to keep Amanda and me away, but that's not how the universe seems to work.

"Don't worry, though, the staff's average life span is nearly forty years, so she will have a long and productive career," he says with a soft laugh.

Amanda doesn't deserve this, but I should have known this is how Magnus gets people to do what they want. Even though Farren brought us to this hell, he was driven by his love for his family. Now I am facing a similar path, a life of manipulating the innocent to protect the only person I have in this world. Consciousness seems to draw in what you put the most focus on. Unfortunately, this can also bring you what you fear the most. And there's nothing more frightening than being alone.

"You better decide soon, she is close to being assigned," Mavis says while looking at one of the displays.

"You will regret this, I promise." I lock on his beady eyes.

"The only thing I regret is not finding you sooner. Every sector group has been trying to find you for the last six years. It just so happened you stumbled upon us, rescuing one of our very own. The board will look favorably upon me for this fortunate discovery."

What happened on the last day at that shelter with those boys from the Southern Alliance was beyond intense for me, but I did not think it would trigger a manhunt for the last six years. Amanda and I have been much luckier than I could've ever dreamed. Unfortunately, my careless act of compassion toward Farren ruined everything for us.

Furious, I can't hold my tongue any longer. "You will regret this. I will find a way to make you pay. You can't hide behind that desk forever."

Wrapped up in anger, I fail to notice the familiar sting that hits my shoulder. A fresh injection of sedative enters my body. Before I drift off, Mavis crouches down to tell me one more thing.

"You are a lucky girl." He pauses. "You are being called up to the top. We are transporting you to Talas to work with the leadership. Your talent will help us expand faster than ever before. You will bring thousands and thousands into our fold."

Mavis slithers away as my vision blurs and my mind yet again drifts. When I awaken, I will be forced to manipulate the lives of countless people. My soul will gradually be lost.

5
IN THE THICK OF IT

THERE'S SOMETHING ABOUT this sedative that makes me aware I am dreaming. I know I'm knocked out on the way to the Magnus headquarters, but my mind is yet again taken back to my early childhood. This time, I catch on a little earlier to the delusion.

It's some sort of overgrown playground where the slides and swing sets are rusted and the grass and bushes hide most of its youthful appearance. I am playing in a dirty sandbox on a small patch of clean sand. There is a sense of complete happiness that is unfamiliar to me. Two grownups are sitting on a nearby bench. One of them is leaning on the other; their gazes locked on each other. It is my parents, I just know it. I try to call out to them, but each time I speak they become blurry and more distant. My memories of what they look like are far too buried for me to recall. I wish I could see their faces so I could have something of my family to hold on to.

An unfocused entity walks up to me, the face covered by that frustrating haze. Outstretched arms reach for me. My whole body is excited to see this being. I open myself up to embrace this illusion when I hear a distorted boy's voice say, "You need to go now."

I am thrown off by the words, as this person feels important to me. I want to stay here, in this moment. Stiff hands grip my shoulders and he shouts, "NOW."

Thrust back to the real world, I find myself trapped in a van with my hands tied in the familiar plastic wrap. Somehow, the intensity of the dream forced me out of my paralyzed state. Alone in the rear of this transport vehicle, I find myself able to move and search for a way out. The quiet hum of the electric motor makes it hard to move around undetected with the two men in the front cabin. Looking out the smudged and cracked windows, I see two other beat-up vehicles following us. Magnus has built up quite the stockpile of these cars and trucks. I need to find a way out of this prison on wheels if I will have any chance of escaping. Next, I'll have to figure out a way to rescue Amanda.

My thoughts jump from thinking of a way to break free, to what my mind is trying to show me with these drug-induced dreams. Why did my subconscious force me to wake at this very moment? Then the answer comes to me.

Suddenly, a massive explosion rattles the vehicle behind ours. It teeters on two wheels before slamming into a washed-out ditch. The shockwave of this blast rocks our van and the driver loses control. A tire pops, suddenly dropping us down. We run off the road into a small, dried-up gulley. The intense impact throws me around the cargo hold just before launching me out a side window. I land several yards from the road in a grove of ferns. Blood flows down my face and arms. The glass from the van's window has left a large gash on the crown of my head. My arms are covered in cuts. I lay back. The pain from my injuries has yet to sink in; the trees above spin and I can see double of everything now.

A minute or two passes and my vision begins to clear. Sounds of gunfire circle where I lay. I realize that someone has attacked our convoy, and now the Magnus personnel are trying to fight them off. Lifting my head, I see two uniformed men pinned down behind the third car that brought up the rear of our group. They are shooting blindly into the woods. One of the men grabs a small communication device from his side pocket and begins relaying the apparent situation to someone.

"We have been ambushed by the Vernon Society," the man shouts over the echoing cracks and hisses from bullets. "They are after the cargo."

Am I the cargo? Are they after me?

The Vernon Society is the sector group that controls most of the Pacific Northwest of the country. They have been at war with the Magnus Order for as long as I can remember. They both rely heavily on Influencers to expand their territories.

In spite of a painful throbbing that pulsates through my head and shoulders, the urgency to take advantage of this chaos and make my escape comes to the forefront. Blood trickles down my arms as I stagger to prop myself up against the nearest tree. The bark of the tree digs into my cuts and forces out a muffled cry. Some broken glass from the crash helps me free my hands from the restraints. Dark red blood stings my eyes as the head wound continues to gush and make its way down the contours of my face. There is no time to take care of myself, I need to run now, but my mind and legs are not on the same page. I can't find the willpower to move from this tree.

Fate steps in when an immense blast booms from the woods where the Vernon Society gunmen are firing. This blast is from a far more powerful weapon than the usual sector pistols and rifles. This is some new tech that I have not come across. A second bang erupts and my resting spot is shattered a few feet above my head. Nearly severed, this thick tree trunk begins to fall. I move just in time as the huge tree rattles the ground.

Crackling twigs and rustling sounds of brush drown out my heavy breathing as I tear through the forest as fast as I can. Pure adrenaline propels me forward even as my injuries sap my body. The gun blasts and sounds of the battle begin to fade the deeper I go into the wilderness.

Thirty minutes or so pass and my legs give out, forcing me to the ground. The idea to just lay here and give up is very tempting, but I have to look out for Amanda, just like she has for me. Several minutes have passed now and the urge to move on kicks in. Wobbly, weak legs make running impossible now, so I drag my body from tree to tree, leaning on each one for a few seconds before I continue on to the next. I'm surrounded by forest so thick the canopy blots out the sun. Has anyone ever been here? Within seconds, I find a cavern at the base of one of the overgrown trees. Sliding down a moss-covered slope, I crouch inside the shallow opening. I'm confident I can stay hidden—but how do I get out of here?

It must be one or two o'clock in the afternoon now, based on where the sun is in the sky. It's been an hour since my escape and my feet slowly drag through vegetation as I inch my way forward. Step after step appears directionless until I stumble across a faint but definite dirt road. Hope pushes back some of the pain and exhaustion; I frantically look in all directions for signs of civilization. Finally, out of the corner of my eye, about three hundred yards north, I spot a small structure at the end of this neglected road. Walking closer, the structure becomes clearer and an abandoned ranger outpost reveals itself to me. I make my way to the front of this weathered-looking gray building that is no more than ten feet across in each direction. The rusty metal handle fails to unlatch. Without hesitation, I grab a large rock and smash a hole in the window near the entrance. *Wow, that was loud.* The dire situation pushes any fear of being found far out of my mind.

Reaching through the window, I find the deadbolt on the inner latch and with all my remaining strength I dislodge the stiff lock. The door creaks open to reveal a cramped room with a small cot on one side, a wood oven on the other wall, and a tall cabinet in the middle propped up against the back. My guess is that no one has been here for years, as dust and dirt cover every inch of the room. Breathing heavily, my eyes narrow in on the cabinet in the hope that there's something of use inside. Pulling on the latch jars it open and desperation turns into relief; it is still packed with supplies.

It's time to address my wounds or there will be nothing at all to worry about anymore. This cabinet has several useful items inside. The first thing that I recognize is a HypoPatch kit, and hope becomes a possibility again. This kit works by spraying some sort of antiseptic bonding agent on the wound and then applying a skin-like, elastic wrap bandage to seal everything. I spray it on the cuts on my arms and instantly I feel the gashes pull together as a tingling sensation crawls over my limbs. I wrap the bandages on my arms and the pain is nearly gone. These wraps have a cooling sensation that is very soothing. Now I need to deal with the more serious injury on my head. Inside the cabinet hangs a small mirror on the door, I lean in to have a peek and cringe at the large gash that has spilled out over the crown of my head. Luckily, it has clotted up a bit and the blood flow is not as intense. Weak and lacking focus from the blood loss, I find it hard to concentrate on what I need to do. I know from the nurse at my last shelter that the HypoPatch will not work on this big a wound, so I scan the contents of the cabinet. Stuffed in the top corner, I find a stem-cell ointment applicator that is about five years past its shelf life.

I remember years ago when Amanda nearly lost her arm while goofing around on a roof and fell on an intake fan. There was a gruesome tear that looked like her forearm was just dangling from her elbow. Somehow, our shelter approved the nurse to use this precious ointment on her. Days later, her arm was good as new.

This treatment is supposed to reconstruct your cells around the wound and regenerate what is damaged. I can only hope this expired treatment will still work. Poured generously, the slimy, orange gel starts to fuse with my open gash. A fizzling sound starts and while looking in the mirror I watch a lighter foam-like substance form over the top of my head. A smell of rotten flowers tickles my nose. The medicine is overtaking the wound and sealing it while it does its magic. I find some food rations hiding in the back and take them to the cot. I flop down on the poorly padded bed and a huge plume of dust floats up a few feet in the air. I'm in desperate need of rest, and I know this ointment requires some time to do its work.

Arms wrapped stiff and my head bubbling over with medicine, I stare at the wall while eating bland turkey and mashed potato flavored food rations. All the thoughts running through my mind are of Amanda stuck at Hawthorne forced to dig holes, or whatever they do in the slave labor division. Not even stress or worrying about this can stop my eyes from rolling back. Conked out and stuck in a handy little ten-by-ten box, ripe for the taking, it doesn't seem like I will ever be able to sleep normally again.

6

A MOMENT OF CHANGE

THE WILL TO survive thrusts me awake and I lean forward. Confused, I take a moment, gather myself, and collect my thoughts. I notice dried streaks of orange powder lining my shoulders and chest. The ointment residue also stains the cot where my head rested. Out the window, through the lush trees that surround this outpost, I see the sun is starting to set. It has already dipped below the treetops. The plan was to rest for a little bit and then move on once I regained enough strength. I must've been out for close to four hours. This is not good. I need to be long gone from this area by now. I brush off the remaining powder from my head and feel a much smoother surface than the jagged and mangled wound that was once there. Food, medicine, and rest have left me full of energy and able to concentrate again. Tucked in the corner of the room I find a small backpack and fill it with whatever is useful from the cabinet: several food rations, another HypoPatch kit, a compass, and a flashlight fill the bag. Just as I turn to leave, I hear someone in the distance shout, "I found something." Fear buckles my legs and I collapse into a corner of the outpost. The beveled metal panels on the wall rattle as I press my back against it.

Peeking out the window, I see several armed Magnus security personnel make their way toward the outpost. *No-no-no, I screwed myself.* Mutterings in the distance increase as they move in. Before long, the oncoming men surround me. Out of the corner of my eye, I catch a glimpse of a tall dark-skinned man walking to a clearing several yards from the entrance of the outpost.

In a commanding, deep voice the man says, "We know you're in there, Kaylin. Although I'm surprised you're still alive with all that blood you've lost."

My head hitting that van window shook me up more than I thought. I can't believe I didn't think to cover my tracks.

They must believe I'm armed or dangerous in some way or they would just storm this shack and take me. Do they know something I don't? Is there a weapon in here somewhere? If Farren was telling the truth, each of them has the implant, so my ability will have no effect on them. I am literally boxed in and helpless.

"There is nowhere to run, little girl, my men surround you now," insists the leader. "You must be aware we're all shielded, so let's just make this easier on everyone and have you come out quietly so no one gets hurt."

I don't want to go back; I can't go back. Amanda needs me to get her out of that hell they've trapped her in. Emotions begin to boil up inside me. I need help from someone and I need it now. "Please, please help me," I mutter to myself with my eyes closed and my body curled in a corner. "Get these men away from me."

I don't know if there is a god or a higher source, but I could use some divine intervention right about now. My emotional state somehow engages my push ability. I feel my inner being stretch out on its own like it's on autopilot. Approaching steps from the Magnus thugs only heighten my push and I feel it expand further than I have ever been able to reach before. My fear locks my mind on the idea of getting these men away from this outpost. I envision them being dragged out into the woods, their eyes terrified as they kick and scream for their lives.

The movements of the men come to a nearly complete stop, their bodies inch forward in slow motion. Time has slowed as the conscious reality surrounding me starts to bind together. A feeling of purity enters the fold and I become connected with what I can only describe as the thoughts and visions of innocent souls. Whoever it is I'm connecting to doesn't have the complexities or the emotional weaknesses of anyone I have ever pushed before. It feels wonderful to be bonded with these pure, conscious entities. Maybe there is a god, and whoever it is sent angels to me. Never before have I been able to keep my focus on the moment while also pushing my will out to others. Slipping back to the current reality feels effortless. Whatever push happened is now complete and time is moving at its familiar rhythm again.

Opening my eyes, I see the Magnus leader peering in through the window into the outpost. Our eyes meet and I can see in his hardened face that he realizes I am nothing more than a weaponless kid, tucked in a fetal position. I need that help now, but I'm in the middle of nowhere grasping at straws.

"We are going to do this the hard way I guess," he snarls.

He reaches his arm back to smash the window when something lunges at him and clamps down on the surprised man's arm. A blur of what looks like fur brushes up against the window. A scream echoes in the clearing and I inch up to see the man's arm being yanked down by a big, tawny-colored creature with claws the size of my fingers and teeth that gleam in the low light. A mountain lion. Shock enters my body and I cover my mouth to hold in my scream.

Two men rush to the leader, ready to fire on the attacking animal when they are knocked together by a full-grown male deer with large antlers. Both men fly to the ground, sliding to a stop at the base of a thick evergreen tree. *What is going on here? Why are these animals going crazy?* Struggling, the man flails as the mountain lion drags him away from my hiding place. The horror of this makes me drop back down to the floor.

Moments later, a loud blast rattles my little shack. Once again, I push myself up the wall that protects me, peeking out the window. The large cat is dead on the ground as blood drips on its face from the mangled arm of the Magnus security boss who now stands over it. The gun remains pointed at the beast when a loud snarl from the surrounding woods snaps the man out of his deadly stance. He steps back and looks for cover, but it's too late. A grizzly bear stampedes out of the foliage and with one lunge the man is smashed to the ground with two massive paws pinning his lifeless body down. A quick gasp leaves my body as another bear flies out from behind the outpost and starts after some retreating Magnus personnel. I turn to see the grizzly bear bite down on a leg of each of the unconscious men that lay near the large tree. The sight of the grizzly must have spooked the deer that bulled them over. The bear easily picks them up and proceeds to carry them into the woods.

It dawns on me; it was my autopilot push. I panicked and reached out for someone to take these men away from me. Those pure spirits that I connected to were not angels; they were animals. I don't understand how this is possible. I have never heard of an Influencer affecting the reality of anything but people. Why am I so different?

Several frenzied whacks hit the locked door. Three men from the Magnus Order beg to enter as more animals fill the area. Distrust keeps me frozen in the corner as I watch a small herd of crazed deer emerge from the far side of the woods searching for prey. It figures—only I could make docile animals like deer turn into predators.

Light is fading fast as the day winds down, making it harder to spot the onslaught of aggressive creatures out for blood.

Bang, bang, bang. Should I let them in? *Bang, bang, bang.* Their knocks become more frantic. I'm just about to get up and let them in when the knocks stop and out the window I watch the men sprint out toward the dirt road. What's going on? I see a pack of what I can only assume are wild dogs chasing after them. Three canines, all different in size and shape, team up to hunt my enemies. Their barks drown out the men's calls for help as they dart deeper into the backdrop. The fleeing men, followed closely by the ravenous pack of dogs, disappear into the woods. Shortly after, I hear screams and howling that make my limbs tremble. If I wasn't so terrified I could concentrate and try to stop this madness, but all I can do is close my eyes and put my hands over my ears while I attempt to block everything out.

The muffled screams and rustling sounds from the woods gradually begin to ease. I build up the strength to look out the window again and find animals dispersing into the backdrop. A large deer walks only a few feet from the outpost window and I swear it nods at me, as if letting me know I am safe now. Did this whole event really just happen? Disbelief fills my thoughts, as the horror I just witnessed is too much to handle.

Several minutes pass and the only sounds I hear are the creaking trees as the wind gently sways them back and forth. It should be safe for me to have a look now, but do I really want to venture outside this structure? I don't want it to be real; it can't be. It is getting dark. There's no choice, I need to go now.

Hands shaking, I take a deep breath and unlock the door. Whatever ounce of security this outpost provided disappears as I peer out and witness something I have never seen before.

Even as the light of day begins to retreat, I am able to see the full horror of yet another life-taking push. The first thing that I notice is the leader's sunken chest as the paws of the grizzly have flattened the life from his body. Not wanting to see, I turn to find the three men that I denied at the outpost door; their bodies lying in the clearing about one hundred yards to the right of where I am. The pack of wild dogs has made them unrecognizable: chunks of flesh torn from their limbs, scratch marks covering their exposed skin. They had no chance to survive. No chance at all. Just off to the side of this blood bath, I see a chewed-up boot and pack from one of the men the grizzly bear dragged into the woods. There's no doubt in my mind their bodies will never be found. The wilderness will consume every piece of them. I wonder how many more ripped-apart bodies lay in the woods from other attacks I didn't see. I drop to my knees, unable to take any more. I look up to the darkening sky and scream. Whatever humanity that is left in me rips out of my throat. The animal-like cry echoes through the woods, but I don't care who hears. My spirit is broken; I don't deserve to be free. I have killed too many people. My hands drop to the ground and I'm about to give up and let the forest reclaim me as well when someone grabs me from behind. A man covers my mouth and wraps his arms around me, pulling me in tight. A shallow breath escapes my mouth, but I don't even react. I simply don't care anymore.

"Please don't scream," he begs. "Kaylin, it's okay."

I can't believe this. It's Farren. His voice brings fire back to my cold and depressed body. Thoughts of revenge fuel my hatred. I replay his betrayal in my head, and at this moment, there is nothing more I want than to take one more life.

7
REINTRODUCTION

I TRY TO wrestle myself free, but Farren's strong arms are impossible to break from. Being this deep in this isolated part of the forest just means no one would hear me scream now.

"Please, stay calm," he pleads. "I'm not here to capture you...or hurt you. Let me explain." I feel him take a deep breath as he slowly removes his hand from my mouth.

"Let go of me, NOW," I demand. "Get your arms off me before you end up like your little Magnus friends." I wince as I take a quick glance at the nearby carnage.

"I'm not with them," he insists. "I heard about the attack on your caravan and I knew this was my opportunity to make things right. Please let me explain."

His grip softens some, but the grasp remains firm and unyielding.

"I don't want to hear your lies," I say, still thrashing. "We saved your life and you threw us on the fire."

"I never intended for this to happen. Please stop fighting so I can talk. If you still think I'm full of it, I'll let you go. I promise."

Knowing I really have no choice, I stop fighting and relax. I can't bear to see another person die by my push, even Farren.

"Say what you have to say, but know I really couldn't care less right now."

"Alright," he sighs. "I'm going to let go of you now, please give me a chance to talk."

I really just want to run from him, but he is faster, stronger, and he is the best tracker the Magnus Order has. Just because he released me from his hold doesn't mean I have any chance of getting away. "Fine. Talk."

He gestures for me to sit down against the outpost wall and I comply. He sits to the right of me and leans his head against the structure, scanning the surrounding area. "Wow, your ability is truly amazing. How was that even possible?"

"Is this what you want to talk about?" I snarl. "I'm not interested in talking about how *awesome* a killer I am."

"Sorry… I'm sorry, I didn't mean to… um, you know—"

"Just say what you came to say."

"Okay, okay. Well, when you found me unconscious, slumped up against that road sign, it wasn't because of poor judgment or bad planning." He breathes in and the exhale seems to release weight from his shoulders. "I was giving up."

"What do you mean 'giving up'?" I ask, genuinely curious despite myself.

"They almost killed my father. I was visiting him that day you found me, and I needed to see firsthand what my actions caused. I can't do this anymore. Recruiting naive people into this group is tearing at my soul."

He drops his head into the palms of his hands, seemingly overwhelmed. "I know I said I don't do that, but sometimes there's no choice. They haven't been pleased with my reluctant performance of late, and they made an example of him. My family refuses to run from our land, so it is all on my shoulders to keep them safe. My mother tries to protect me by telling me they will be fine, but they won't—not as long as I keep disappointing Magnus."

Farren's head drops deeper into his hands as the pain overcomes him. His hard exterior is cracked and I can see he's just an eighteen-year-old boy that was forced to grow up way too fast. I know what it is like to be robbed of a normal childhood. I've seen firsthand what Magnus has done to people who fail to meet their expectations. Innocents beaten to death for defying them is not uncommon. Known as one of the most ruthless sector groups in the area, I have steered as far away from them as possible. Now I am stuck in the middle of this Magnus hell.

"I'm done with this crap," he snarls. "I had it all worked out. I thought if I brought you in, I would be able to help you escape in a day or so. I came up with a whole plan that night, but I didn't know you were the girl everyone has been looking for." His reaction looks genuine. "I didn't know they would transport you to Talas the same day I brought you in. It normally takes days for people to be sorted and reassigned. I thought I could save everyone... my family, you and Amanda, myself—everyone."

I don't know if I can really believe him. I barely know him. Ever since we met a few days ago, my life has gone from bad to worse.

"You used me as a pawn," I say. "Why did you even come here to find me? You protected your family by bringing me in. They won't blame you for what happened after you *delivered* me. Why are you here now?"

He leans forward, sweat dripping from his tightened brow. "I want to make things right with you and Amanda, but there's something bigger going on and we need your help."

My help? Is he losing his mind? Who does this guy think he is? I laugh, the sound forced and harsh. "Who's we, and why should I help you?"

"Because, I want to end the Magnus Order, and I think we can do it with the help of your abilities," he says. "I am part of a resistance that has been growing for the last six months. We've been quietly building support and becoming more operational of late. It's time for this corruption to end."

All this time on the road hiding with Amanda has been my life for the last six years, and now he wants me to risk our lives for him and some sort of resistance. He's out of his mind. I'm just about to tell him that he's crazy when I'm interrupted. "I'm going to help you get Amanda back. I just need you to meet with some people first. They will help us free her even if you decide not to join the resistance. But I do need their help, so you will have to hear them out."

My stomach churns, so I stand up to walk off the fear and anxiety that has bubbled to my throat. I pace back and forth in front of Farren as his eyes follow in anticipation of my next move.

"Was that your rebels or whatever you call yourselves who attacked the caravan that was transporting me?"

"No," he says. "Word has spread that Magnus found you. The Vernon Society knows what a find like you could mean for the conflict. I can't believe I didn't put it together when you took out those Harvesters. Why didn't you change your name when you went on the run all those years ago?"

"I was eleven when Amanda and I left. We were kids; we didn't think there would be a manhunt for me. All I knew was that I had to stay on the move and keep my ability to myself. I knew I was different from most Influencers, but I didn't think anyone would care after a few days."

"You don't get it, Kaylin. Your push ability is far beyond what normal Influencers can do. You can instantly change the conscious minds of those around you. There is no need to nurture the push, no need for personnel to meddle in the daily lives of citizens. What you want to happen just happens. And now you can push animals too—truly mind-blowing. You have to know that sector groups like Magnus will never stop hunting you down."

The thought of being on the run, knowing there will be people actively looking for me, does make his offer seem like it's my only option. It's hard for me to get past his betrayal, but I don't think I have a choice if I want to rescue Amanda. I can't do it alone. I stand quietly with my arms crossed as I think of what to do. Options are limited for me and hope is at an all-time low.

"Okay, I will go with you, but if Amanda is hurt I won't hesitate to send hawks to peck out your eyes."

Just the thought of what I say sends chills down my spine and the lump in my throat returns. I don't think I can ever get used to hurting people.

"Thank you," he whispers. "I will earn your trust back, I promise. We need to get moving before they start to wonder what happened."

I reach out to help him up. His hand swallows mine and I struggle to assist him to his feet. Farren is much more of a man than he should be for his age. Once on his feet, he scans our surroundings. He gestures to a path just behind the outpost and I reluctantly agree to follow.

"Where are we going?" I ask.

"There's an abandoned hub a few miles from here. I'll be able to contact Jax and Caiden from there."

More strangers I have to worry about, more unknowns to figure out. Life was empty before, but at least it was fairly safe and easy.

"I hope you can trust these people."

"They have been with me since the beginning. I've known them for a long time now. Jax is the leader of the resistance and will come up with a plan for getting Amanda out of Hawthorne. They are really good people."

I guess I assumed Farren would be the leader of this resistance. He has a commanding personality and is determined to get things done. This Jax guy better come up with a rescue plan or I will be lost.

"Good people do bad things, too." I look up at him to see if he caught my little jab.

Without looking back he replies, "I'm glad you see that I'm a good person."

"Well... uh." I stop and shake my head. Damn, I didn't mean for it to come out like that, but I guess I do see him as a good person after all. I hope I am right, but still... He doesn't need to know that.

I gather the salvaged supplies from the ranger outpost before I move on to the path. Taking one more look at the death I've caused, I cringe. I don't deserve to forget this. I take extra long to soak it all in before I return to Farren at the edge of the road. We cut through a faint, overgrown path for several minutes, not saying a word.

Looking up, the moon catches my attention as the daylight fades into the backdrop of the forest. This moon also lit our way as we traveled to Bullhead together last night. It reminds me of my first conversation with Farren. He seemed so sincere. Was it all an act? Or did he really not know I was this special Influencer prize that the world was looking for?

About thirty minutes into our trek through the woods, we come to a small stream. Farren suggests we stop to rest. I do not argue with him, as my head wound has been throbbing for several minutes now. The trickling sounds of the flowing water seem so peaceful. I almost forget about the pain and all the uncertainties that lie ahead. After filling a small canteen, he comes to my side and kneels next to me.

Noticing the ugly dried blood and ointment on my head, Farren asks, "Can I take a look at your head? Are you in any pain?"

"Oh… um… I have a headache," I say, rubbing my temples. "I'll be okay."

"Well, let me see how it's healing," he insists.

Farren moves behind me, grabbing both arms, and gently pulls me back against his chest. I slump forward at first, but eventually I relax and lean back on him. He is a solid guy. His body covers mine and I feel protected from the outside world. His hands run through my hair as he examines the wound. It feels nice. My doubts about him begin to wash away. I don't want to be that gullible girl whenever a guy treats me kindly, but something about him makes me feel safe.

"It's healing nicely, I barely see anything."

"What?" I blurt out while not paying attention. "Oh…yeah, that's good."

Come on, Kaylin, don't lose focus.

"Let's clean up this rat's nest," he smirks, picking at my crusty mane.

"Shut up," I hiss.

He laughs. "No really, come on. I'll help you wash it out."

He guides me to the narrow creek, which is no more than a few feet across. I get on my hands and knees and lean over it. Farren uses his canteen to rinse out the clumpy residue. His hands squeeze out the grime as he pulls the water from the ends of my hair. I'm beyond due for a trim. My hair nearly reaches my backside, and bugs the crap out of me. Amanda is the one who takes care of the grooming. Whenever she gets her hands on my wavy locks, she throws it up into unique ponytails. I miss her now more than ever.

"Do you think she's okay?" I ask. "They won't hurt Amanda, will they?"

"I don't know, but you can bet she is being heavily guarded since your escape. We will save her; I won't rest till I make this right."

He hands me a shirt from his pack and tells me to dry up. It has that recognizable Farren smell. I'm not sure why I really know what Farren's smell is, but the subtle hint of sawdust reminds me of when Amanda and I dragged his unconscious body off the road when we first found him. I bet it's from working on his family's ranch in Lost Souls.

"We better get going," he suggests.

Another thirty minutes of being poked and scraped by branches while we travel leads us to a clearing that is masked by darkness. The tall evergreen trees that tower all around this clearing block out most of the moonlight. I can hardly see ten yards in front of me. We walk several paces into this vast space when out of nowhere an immense structure begins to reveal itself to us. Crumbling walls that reach five stories delicately lean against one another for support.

"What is this?" I ask. "What happened here?"

"This is what's left of the Walton hub," he says. "It was part of the Magnus network before it was destroyed by the Vernon Society a few years back. Come on, let's get inside so we can contact the others."

He grabs my hand and leads me around the side of the hub to a slanted, rusted metal entrance. It resembles the opening to a fallout shelter from when people worried about nuclear war. Forty or fifty years ago, governments would use these weapons for fear, but Amanda told me that early Influencers played a part in ridding the world of them. Whoever built these hubs in the past must have made a killing selling to all the desperate moguls who once ruled the world.

We hunch over to avoid hitting our heads on the low ceiling and move down through a hollow-sounding staircase. Our footsteps clank and echo as we move toward a dim light in the distance. The closer we get, the more I can recognize an opening with several closed doors on all sides. The dim red light comes from an emergency fixture above the open door. The air smells of mildew and there's a strong smell of something rotting. If there was ever a place where you needed to be left alone or undiscovered, this would be it. It's beyond gross and creepy.

"Over here," Farren says, clearing away spider webs above my head as we enter the room. "There is a fairly clean cot over there. You'll need your rest for tomorrow. I'll have them meet us at dawn."

Farren turns on a small, battery-powered lantern that he finds on a metal desk that's next to the bed. The space is no bigger than the shelter bedroom Amanda and I shared six years ago. I clearly remember that bedroom because it was the first time I was able to bunk with only one other child. I felt grown up. Shelters would stuff as many young kids in one room as they could. That was the last time either of us had a place to call our own.

Farren rolls out a small stool from under the desk to sit on. From a small black box he pulls out some sort of a communication device that I've never seen before. He tells me the device piggybacks on an unused Magnus frequency band. It then sends data in small waves so the communication will look like simple background noise. Not ideal for long conversations, but perfect for covert messages.

"Hopefully, you will meet Owen Helix," he says with a smile. "He's our tech specialist, who invented this device and a ton of other gear. He's brilliant, but quite a character."

I lie down on the cot, resting my head on my hand as I watch him operate the device. "Echo one—pantry full—party starts—0600," he parses into the device. It is some sort of coded message.

Whatever he thinks this party is going to be, it better include saving Amanda or he is attending it alone.

8

RESISTANCE

I DON'T REMEMBER falling asleep, but I was beyond tired. Morning comes too soon as I rub the cloudiness from my eyes. I regain focus and notice a large cardboard box next to the bed where Farren sat last night. All sorts of random clothes fill the tattered container. The box is labeled 'Walton Lost and Found.' Farren knows I've been wearing the same outfit for the last few days. I don't smell the best and the layer of grime is getting unpleasant. My first reaction should be relief that I get to clean up a bit, but I'm more embarrassed than anything else. I find a black T-shirt and a pair of jeans that look like they should fit well. I wish there was a working shower here, rinsing off at the stream last night is not cutting it. I quickly throw on the clothes, and instantly feel better. The used outfit feels brand new and somehow has a smell of innocence. Recently washed clothes have a scent that reminds me of normalcy. Life was simple back in the shelters. It still sucked, but at least I wasn't a wanted prize for the greedy.

The partially latched metal door creaks open as I enter the corridor. A faint and familiar smell tickles my nose. *What is that?* It's savory, and I know I've had it before. A reflective metal panel on the wall makes for a makeshift mirror. I look horrible, but at least the wound on my head has healed and there are no signs of any cut ever being there. Using a pencil I found on the desk in my room, I put my hair into a sloppy bun and try to find where the yummy smell is coming from. The dungeon-like odor of the hallway is nearly covered by the smell—the key word being 'nearly.'

Light bounces off the corridor walls from an outside source and brightens my path. I follow the smell and find Farren in a small kitchen at the far side of the structure. Quietly, I lean in the doorway without him noticing. I watch him as he cooks breakfast. He knows what he's doing as he works a frying pan and spatula.

"Shut up—are those eggs you're cooking?" I blurt out.

He jumps and nearly flips the food on the ground. "Geez, Kay, I almost burned myself."

"Sorry." I smile.

"I wish they were real eggs," he says. "They're synthetic powder eggs *fresh* from the bag. Just add water."

He just called me Kay. I haven't heard anyone except Amanda call me that. It has a nice ring coming from him.

"Sit down. We have about twenty minutes before they get here."

"Yes, sir," I say with a salute and a grin.

We sit across from each other and eat our fake eggs as we wait for more members of this resistance. I don't know if this rebel group using Influencers is really any better than Magnus and the other sector groups using us.

"Do you really think your resistance can take on Magnus?" I ask. "They have so many weapons and Influencers."

"That's the plan. If you help us, we have a real chance at ending their corruption."

"What do you think I'm going to do?" I ask. "I can't kill any more people... I just can't."

Farren stands and takes his food tin and fork to the sink. He turns to me with his head down. "You know we can't defeat evil just by wishing it. Sometimes things get ugly, but reward takes great sacrifice. Just hear Jax out, okay?"

"Who is this Jax guy anyway?" I take my last bite and hand him the tin.

With a quick rinse, it goes on a drying rack to the side of the sink. He leans back on the counter and crosses his legs. His deep brown eyes focus on me as he says, "Jax is the head Influencer for Magnus."

"What!" I jump to my feet and start toward the door. "How could you do this to me—again?"

He clutches my hand and pulls me back to him. "No, wait. It's not what you think. He has his own issues with Magnus. He's been building this resistance from within. Jax puts his life at risk every day by staying close to the inner workings of the leadership. I trust him with my life."

"I don't know about this anymore," I say. "This is getting more and more shady, and you're already on a short leash with me as it is."

All I can think is, *How do I get out of this?* I've made the wrong choice—and probably signed both my and Amanda's death warrants in doing so. But what choice do I have now? I could—

A frazzled buzz startles me out of my panicked musings. What the hell is that?

"They're here," he says. "That's the entrance alert. Please just hear him out, okay?"

"I really have no choice now, do I?" I say, arms crossed and my jaw set.

Farren and I head to the entrance hatch to meet them. I take a deep breath and exhale, as if that will do anything to stop my legs from shaking. He opens the door and the light shimmering off the morning dew nearly blinds us. The cool, crisp air is unfamiliar to me. Lost Souls has only two climate changes: hot and very hot. Two young figures emerge from the light. One guy, who looks twenty-something, has bright-red hair and wears a torn military uniform that must be fifty years old. Somebody must really love combat. Then there is the other boy, who looks as young as Farren, but his blue eyes look much older than his face. They look like they have seen the sorrow of countless victims, and that weight has been etched into his irises. He stares right at me and instantly I am uncomfortable. I lower my head, sure he can somehow pull the thoughts right through my eyes.

Pointing to the red-haired guy, Farren smiles and says, "This serious-looking dude is Caiden Rushmore. He is our tactical genius and war nerd."

"Hey!" barks Caiden. "This nerd will knock that smile right off your face, *Ferret*."

A subtle laugh escapes as I watch Farren and Caiden playfully attack each other in the clearing. I turn to see Jax extending his hand my way. "Hi, Kaylin," he says softly. "My name is Jax Riley. I've heard a lot about you."

His voice is clear and calming. I know he is not using his ability on me, as Influencers can't push other Influencers, but it still feels as if he is putting me at ease somehow.

"Hey. Nice... uh... nice to meet you, too."

"Thanks for giving me a chance to talk to you," he says, shaking my hand firmly. "Your ability is becoming well known throughout Magnus. I'm glad you were able to escape before they placed you at your post. I can imagine what they would force you to do."

The life of tinkering in people's reality for the greedy purposes of the Magnus Order would be a far worse fate than death.

"I really don't want to imagine that, to tell you the truth," I say. "Let's just pretend they'd have me washing dishes. I hate doing dishes."

I swear I can almost see him crack a slight smile. "Yeah, me too," he says, releasing my hand.

My legs have stopped shaking and the uncertainty surrounding him has eased a bit.

"Do you mind if I ask where Magnus found you?"

He looks over to Farren and Caiden, who are laughing as they walk back to the dilapidated hub. He raises his hand at Farren as if to tell him he and I will join them soon. Farren nods, then glances at me with a thoughtful look. He knows I'm not the most comfortable with this situation. I give him a soft smile as he disappears down the hatch opening.

"Think we can take a walk?" he asks. "I'll fill you in."

I swallow, but nothing happens as nerves have robbed me of any moisture in my mouth. "Yeah, okay," I say reluctantly.

We begin walking around the hub. I notice the battle scars that are covering the outer walls. It is a clear reminder of how cruel the world is now. Fighting just to expand and be bigger than the next group. It's just sad how little we have learned from the collapse of society so long ago.

"This area still takes my breath away," he explains while scanning the lush, green-filled backdrop. "These trees and the natural beauty are so different from where we grew up."

"You're from Lost Souls?"

"Yeah, I was recruited at sixteen. Before that, I hadn't been anywhere else. I wouldn't have left if it wasn't for the Vernon Society taking my parents. That changed everything."

We continue walking along the edge of the clearing. "Why did they take your parents?"

"Well, I wasn't the most well-behaved kid when I was younger," he confesses. "My push ability was exploding at the time, and I wouldn't hesitate to show it off."

He tells me how he would use his push on people in his town to guide them to become 'extra generous' toward him. Soon people were treating him like some sort of boy king, and this behavior did not go unnoticed.

"My parents knew the recruiters would come for me," he says. "I was stupid and didn't think about anyone but myself. They tried to teach me how to act responsibly, but I didn't listen. Shortly after my fifteenth birthday is when they came for me."

Confused, I ask, "Why did the Vernon Society take your parents instead of you?"

"We caught wind of them coming days in advance," he says. "I didn't waste any time. I molded the town into a small army ready to fight for my family, but there would be no fight. I didn't even know they left, I was too caught up in my own little rebellion to notice."

"Who left?" I ask.

"My parents. They left early that morning to cut off the Vernon Society before they got to town. They never came back."

Jax stops and sits down on an old, rotting tree stump. He looks like he's fighting back years of emotion. "Sorry... I don't normally talk about this."

"No, it's okay. It must have been hard to lose your parents like that."

I don't want to make him uncomfortable, but I can't help trying to figure him out.

"How did you end up with Magnus then?" I ask, inching closer to him.

"Months of depression and anger took its toll on me," he admits. "After my parents were taken I rarely left my living unit. I vowed to never use my ability on innocent people again, but it wasn't until a Magnus recruiter visited our town that I decided to break that vow. I knew Magnus and the Vernon Society had been at war with each other for years. Sitting at home crying myself to sleep each night was not going to get my parents back. I decided the best thing I could do would be to help Magnus take down the Society. It was simple to me at the time. Destroy them, and hope my parents are still alive."

I find a free spot next to him on the tree stump and sit. He looks at me with a simple smile. His eyes radiate compassion and his whole being seems to give off a sense of ease. I lean over so I can meet his gaze. "Are you using your push ability on me? I mean... I sense something that I have not felt before."

A controlled laugh pushes out as he angles his head toward me. "That's funny, I was going to say the same thing to you. But I don't think it's possible for Influencers to push other Influencers."

Even after years of doing the dirty work for Magnus, he still has the look of a kid. His short buzz haircut does little to change this fact. He's tall and good looking like Farren, but he carries himself differently and I just can't put my finger on what it is.

"So tell me, why spend so many years with Magnus only to turn on them like this?" I ask. "Wasn't the point of joining them to take down the Vernon Society?"

"Well, when I was first recruited they quickly discovered how effective my push ability was," he says. "Within months, I was made head Influencer due to my ability to alter the reality of so many people at once. The leadership was so pleased with my skills that they started to focus on expansion rather than taking down the Vernon Society. It became a race to grow the fastest. No longer were they concentrating on tactical battles to cripple them, rather they wanted to push them into a corner and make them insignificant." His posture stiffens. "Over the last couple of years, Magnus grew so fast because of me that I found myself losing my soul. I couldn't do it anymore. I lost hope that I would ever get the chance to free my parents from the Vernon Society's stranglehold. It was an endless cycle of doing evil to justify an ever-fading chance to free them. Magnus became the enemy to me and taking them down became the right thing to do."

The conversation seems to drain him a bit and he suggests we head back to the hub. The morning mist has evaporated, exposing a beautiful clear day with sunlight exploding through the trees. The air is so fresh here that it makes you wonder how anyone can bear living in the scorching landscape of Lost Souls. Thinking of this reminds me of Amanda and how we have never been apart for this long before. We would probably be planning our next supply run by now. We always allow for a moment of gorging when we've just stocked up. If you just live life looking for the next food opportunity, you risk losing any piece of humanity you have left. Because of this, we always try to make time for a little slice of fun. Besides, it's one of my favorite things we do. It's a chance to just enjoy life for a second.

"If you don't mind I would like to continue this discussion with the other guys," he suggests.

We make our way down the hub entrance and through the corridor that leads to the kitchen. Caiden sits at the small table devouring a handful of ration packs while Farren leans back on the chair across from him. I notice Farren's rugged scruff. The youth in his face is covered by a day or so of not shaving. Recognizing we've returned, Farren quickly stands and offers me his chair. This gesture makes me uncomfortable. I have never been the kind of girl who gets special attention.

"Okay, guys, it's time to get down to business," Jax says with a determined look. "She knows my story, but we need to fill her in about the resistance. I trust her, but I think she needs to know about us if she is going to help. Caiden, can you run down the logistics?"

"Yes, sir," he says playfully, wiping crumbs from his mouth. "Our resistance consists of eleven Influencers with varying skill sets; twelve implanted, former Magnus members; and fifty-three, influence-free civilians who are sympathetic to our cause. We have amassed a respectable stockpile of weapons as well as three repurposed electric vehicles. Our leadership consists of the three of us here as well as an Influencer named Maddux Rivers and a high-level Magnus personnel coordinator named Miya Hurley. All resistance members who aren't infiltrating Magnus are at secure locations waiting for orders."

"Well... uh... That sounds good, I guess." I start chewing on my bottom lip.

All this rebellion talk makes me uncomfortable. Never before have I been involved in anything this important. I really don't know what I should say.

"I know this is a lot to absorb, Kay," Farren says as he touches my shoulder. "We hope you are willing to help us."

"Listen, Kaylin," Jax says as he moves to Farren's side. "You've seen what sector groups like Magnus do.

Amanda's freewill is being stripped away as we speak. People all over this region suffer every day at the hands of these evil bastards. None of them, including Amanda, deserve that kind of life."

Jax's words show why he is the leader of this resistance. He understands more than anyone that greed and the lust for power only lead to suffering for the innocent.

Caiden sits across the table waiting for my reaction. Jax falls back to the wall next to the kitchen door; his eyes scan everyone in the room. Farren removes his hand from my shoulder and rests it firmly on his side. I suppose this is what it would be like to be the shiny new toy on Christmas morning. Not that I have ever had a Christmas morning—or any holiday, for that matter.

"What do you expect me to do for this resistance?" I ask.

"We need your powerful push ability to help crush Magnus' stranglehold on the area," Caiden says, fists clenched on the table.

"We need your help to free the people controlled by Magnus," Jax says giving Caiden a stern glare. "Your level of involvement is completely up to you, Kaylin."

"Kay," Farren says in a reassuring voice. "It's not going to be easy, but if we don't make a stand now, no one will."

Images of those young shelter bullies barely breathing and bludgeoned lying in pools of their own blood fill my thoughts. As that memory recedes, that awful night we were confronted by the evil Harvesters jumps to the forefront. The way I was able to make them turn on each other gives me chills. That night didn't even compare to the horror I felt when I unleashed wild animals on the Magnus security forces who were hunting me down. The image of the mauled and trampled victims strewn across the forest floor burns the back of my mind. How can I use my push ability again? I'm not an Influencer—I'm a heartless killer. I have spilled enough blood. I just can't do it again. That is when I think of Amanda, alone and forced to live a shortened life of backbreaking labor. She will never be free again. She will be stripped of the chance to experience a full and untethered life. Already filled with so much loss and devastation, she doesn't deserve any more.

"Okay, I'm in, under one condition," I say. "We have to rescue Amanda first."

9
PUSH RADAR

I WISH WE could go back outside. The Walton hub is located in such a beautiful area with all these lush trees, and the fresh air feels so nice with every breath. Jax thinks it would be best if we keep our meetings inside to avoid Magnus patrols. I can't remember a time I've had to be inside this much. It's making me nervous and jumpy. Life was familiar when Amanda and I were wandering Lost Souls. There's nothing fun about the unknown with my current situation. The thought of joining this resistance without all the details on how we plan to take down the evil Magnus Order is frightening, but the only thing on my mind right now is Amanda.

The guys are planning her rescue and my head is spinning. I'm not designed for the war strategizing that Caiden seems to live for. He is going on about a full-on strike on Hawthorne, but Farren is convinced that would be a mistake. A stealth mission with just a few people is his plan, but Caiden is fighting hard for his more aggressive option.

"Caiden, you know I love you, man, but I think Farren is right," Jax says. "A full-on attack on Hawthorne would leave us unprepared for our Talas objective. Once we move on the central hub, our embedded operatives will have to be pulled out. We aren't ready for that yet."

Earlier, Jax told me he's still acting as the head Influencer, but he and the others plan to leave at the very last minute so Magnus would be scrambling to fill the gaps. A major attack like what Caiden is pushing for would signal the start of everything.

"Jax, you need to get back before they start suspecting something," Farren says as he grabs an expired protein bar from the small pantry in the corner of the room. "Kaylin, Caiden, and I can meet up with Maddux on the way back to Hawthorne. We will be in and out in fifteen minutes."

Jax agrees that he should get back to start preparations for the next stage. After some brief goodbyes, Jax leaves and we start gathering supplies to head out soon. It's still early morning and we only have a few hours to travel to get back to Hawthorne. This will leave plenty of time to plan things out.

Tucked away in a small metal cabinet, in one of the rooms on the far side of the Walton hub's lower levels, Caiden pulls out a silver pistol and hands it to me as if I am one of his eager soldiers. My push ability has been the only weapon Amanda and I have ever needed. A gun just draws negative attention, and that is one thing we avoided more than anything else. I'm deadly enough as it is; I don't need any more killing options at my disposal.

"I'll pass," I say, handing back the gun. "Sorry, it's just not my style."

I hope I played that off cool. I don't want to look like some scared little girl to these guys.

"Yeah, I guess you don't need one." Caiden grins. "From what I've heard, you are pretty badass with those mind powers."

"Thanks for the vote of confidence," I say sarcastically. "Come on, let's see if Farren is ready to go."

We find Farren back in the kitchen and begin to assess our gear. He seems to be more serious now that we have a mission at hand. He barely acknowledges me and just goes about his business. After several minutes of him shifting and moving things around, I ask, "Are you alright?"

"Yeah, I'm fine. I just don't want to put you in danger again, that's all. You have to promise me that you'll stay back and do what I say, okay?"

He truly looks concerned about me. It feels nice, but I'm not sure why he would be. According to him, his number-one priority has always been to take down Magnus in order to keep his family safe.

"Okay, but just so you know, I'm going to do whatever it takes to get Amanda out of there."

"I know," he says. "But you have to understand, we can't just send an untrained—"

"An untrained what—girl?" I snap.

"Fighter. I was going to say fighter."

"Oh… sorry," I say, diverting my eyes from him.

Maybe he cares for me as a person or maybe he just doesn't want to lose his new weapon. I'm not quite sure.

He thrusts his pack over his shoulder and leads us down the dim corridor and out of the hub. We enter the clearing to find it has warmed up quite a bit in the hour or so since Jax left to return to Talas. Caiden takes the lead as we head into the lush forest. He tells us we will have to travel west to a camp at the base of the mountains that's about an hour away. It lies in a gap inside the Magnus network of hubs, just out of the reach of the group's Influencers and security patrols. There we will meet up with Maddux, who will help us rescue Amanda from the Hawthorne hub.

As we walk on a faint trail that splinters through the woods, I match Farren's pace and ask, "So tell me about Maddux, who is he?"

"Maddux is a real good guy," he says. "He joined the resistance a few months ago and has been recruiting other Influencers for us. He's originally from the coastal communities."

Amanda and I heard about pockets of people who would move from beach to beach. They would stock up on food and supplies and then move on to the next spot. The coastal areas are way too close to the Harvester-infested inner cities. These large cities were overrun by the worst of humanity shortly after the collapse of society. Now they are just corroded shells with very little water and food. The only things that thrive are the deviants who run all about causing trouble. The sector groups have stayed out of the coastlines for good reason. If there is one thing worse than a sector group, it would be the ruthless Harvesters. The coastal communities have mastered the art of staying on the move, always clinging close to the resource-rich shorelines.

"How did he find you guys?" I ask.

"He was tired of being on the move all the time," he says, sidestepping loose rocks on the trail. "He ventured out looking for others like himself. Influencers who wanted to use their ability to create a free and functional society." He dabs the sweat from his brow with his sleeve before continuing. "Jax and I found him while we were looking for people sympathetic to our cause. He's been huge for our recruiting process due to his ability."

"What is it exactly that he can do?"

"It's pretty cool if I say so myself," Farren says. "He can sense a person's emotional state. Like if they are angry or plotting something or even if they are depressed and losing hope. Things like that. Even better, he can feel when Influencers are using their push ability nearby. Basically, he's a Push radar."

"That's pretty cool," I say, managing to stay a half step behind him.

Time appears to slow as we make our way down a brutal, narrow trail. I'm sure we've been walking for more than an hour now. The forest thins as we reach the lower elevations. The mighty evergreen trees that towered over us now make way for a variety of smaller brush and vegetation. My knees ache as we move down a steep hillside that leads to a small clearing. Caiden points toward a rocky outcrop that covers the far edge of the hill. Several tents and tattered wooden structures are set up near a large cave opening. People are milling about working on different projects. A few people are patching torn outfits while others clean weapons. There are even children running around the camp.

"What is this place?" I ask Caiden. "Are these people all part of the resistance?"

"Yup," he says. "This is one of five camps we have spread over the sector. To be on the safe side, we don't want everyone located in the same place. Everyone is preparing for the war, or...I mean... the confrontation."

It's obvious what he's trying to do by using softer words, but I can tell it's hard for him to hold back his excitement.

This resistance is much bigger and more organized than I thought it was. The reality of the situation is sinking in now and it feels overwhelming, but all I need to do is think of Amanda and my focus snaps back into place.

People stare at us as we pass their tents. Children grab the hands of the nearest adult while others simply stop their work to soak us in. I watch their eyes and notice they're only looking at me, the new girl. People taking notice of me was always the first indication that Amanda and I needed to leave. Avoiding suspicion was a never-ending part of our existence before we met Farren.

We head toward the cave opening when a guy with a black Mohawk and tattoos all over his exposed skin comes out of the darkness. "Welcome. I'm so glad you made it here safely. You must be Kaylin. My name is Maddux. Come on in and get something to eat and drink."

His well-mannered attitude doesn't fit his tatted and gritty appearance. He is older than a lot of the Influencers I know, but not by much—most likely in his early twenties. His hair is pitch black and his skin appears to be deeply tanned by the sun. Tribal markings cover the sides of his closely buzzed head, revealing a possible Native American heritage. The straight strands of his narrow Mohawk flop from side to side as he moves.

We enter the large cave to find makeshift bedding all along the base of the walls. This cavernous space looks like it can shelter at least a dozen people. With the tents outside and the beds in here, there must be twenty or more people on site at the camp. We're led to the back of the cave, where we find a small table with some unfamiliar tech devices on it, all surrounded by metal folding chairs.

"Welcome to South Camp," Maddux says.

"Thanks," I say.

"We got your message this morning," he says, shifting his attention to Farren. "So it looks like someone needs to be rescued?"

Farren is just about to detail his plan when a tall woman enters the cave. Her wavy dark hair is neatly gathered in a ponytail that reaches down to her backside. The most striking thing about her is the white tattoos that intricately spiral up and down her dark skin. She's beautiful like the girls on the cover of those old clothing magazines. She struts up to Maddux and puts her arm around his waist.

"Maddy, you didn't tell me we were going to have visitors so soon."

"Hey, babe," Maddux says with a huge smile. "Guys, this special gal is Ava Reed. I found this superhero taking on Harvesters in old Los Angeles a little over a month ago. She was looking to do some good with her ability and decided to join us. Now she is my beautiful, super queen."

"So you're an Influencer," Caiden says. "What can you do?"

Ava turns to Caiden, her eyes intense. Stepping toward him, she gets within inches of his face and replies, "I specialize in the fear of the weak. There is something about the feeling of a person in terror that excites me. I intensify what haunts people the most and use it against them."

Caiden struggles to maintain his tough-guy appearance as he steps back.

A creepy smile stretches from corner to corner. She then closes her eyes and mutters, "I smell your fear and... it smells like body odor."

Maddux and Ava burst into laughter as Caiden looks on, confused. Farren and I catch on and laugh as well.

"Oh, very funny," Caiden says, his cheeks turning bright red. "This chick looked like she was going to extract my soul for a snack."

Ava steps back into the arms of Maddux and says, "Sorry about that, I couldn't resist."

Fun aside, I find myself curious about her and this push ability she jokes about. "Can you really do that with your ability?" I ask.

"Yeah," she says, the humor gone. "I've been fine-tuning it for fifteen years now. Practice makes perfect."

"Fifteen years?" I say, confused. "How old are you?"

"Twenty-seven years young!" She winks at me.

"How is that possible?" I ask. "I've always been told Influencer's push ability fades as we get into our twenties."

"I don't know what to tell you—I must be special." She shrugs and smiles.

Maddux pulls Farren and Caiden over to the table to show them some type of resistance report. Ava and I continue our conversation. "So, it seems like what you do to other people doesn't bother you," I say. I don't look at her, pretending to focus instead on rolling a thread that dangles from my shirt.

"Kaylin, right?" she asks.

I nod my head.

"Listen." Her face gets more serious. "I believe we were given this power for a reason, and that our freewill shapes us. So, if I'm trying to make the world a better place, I have to use my gift and sometimes using it might lead to someone getting hurt. If we're truly reality creators like we've been told, then our job is to weed out the bad elements to bring about a more pure world. All life is connected, but when the selfish corrode our bond for greedy purposes, then reality becomes fractured and the good of humanity is diluted."

Her thoughts reflect her age, that is for sure, but I doubt anyone has experienced the horrors that I have in such a short period of time. I wish I could have some of her confidence. Life right now would be easier to deal with if I did.

"Hey, sweetie." She rests her hand on my shoulder. "I've heard your story and I know what you've gone through. You have to understand something. We all share this collective experience called life. Everyone affects and molds reality, not just Influencers. What happens to someone is a result of cause and effect. Simply put, we all get what we give, in a sense. Bad people will have bad things happen to them. Don't sweat it anymore, love."

She smiles and heads over to the table with the rest of them. There's a struggle going on inside my mind. One part of me is holding onto the pain as a form a punishment for what I have done. While the other side is trying to let go of it so I can grow into something more. What that something is, I really don't know.

I sink into a creaky chair at the end of the table and listen to them discuss options for this mission. Looks like Maddux and Ava will be rounding out the rescue group. I don't think Farren wants me involved in this mission, as they plan it without even asking for my *expert* advice. From what I pick up, the plan is to cause a subtle diversion and then draw Amanda to a place where we can grab her. I really don't care what the plan is; I just want her back already.

I can't stop thinking about what Ava said to me. Before I met her, all I could think about was the pain I've caused to so many lives. I barely know her, but there's a way about her that makes me question my deep personal guilt.

Pushing down my jitters, I sit up in my seat. "I know you guys think I shouldn't be involved in this mission," I say. "I get it, but this is my friend and I'm done hiding."

The group at the table all turn to me trying to digest what I've said. Caiden turns to Farren with a look of eager excitement. He's been ready to see what I can do since we first met.

"I don't think it's a good idea," says Farren as he avoids Caiden's glare. "You're not a trained Influencer."

"It's not your call," I say. "If you want me to help this resistance, I need to make sure Amanda is safe. I don't know any of you that well. I'm not about to leave her life in the hands of strangers. I'm going."

"Ava and I were never trained," says Maddux. "Her ability has to find its own opportunities to blossom. Each one of us are different."

"We will watch her back," Ava adds.

Outnumbered, Farren has no choice but to agree. And just like that, I'm in.

After a quick lunch of dehydrated rabbit, fern fiddleheads, and some overripe forest berries, we start gathering our things for our two-hour hike on to Hawthorne. I take a deep breath and then release as much of the guilt about the past as I can. Meeting Ava has helped me realize that if I'm going to be of any help on this mission, I can't hesitate because of emotional weakness. Amanda needs me strong now more than ever. It's time to test out what I can really do. Even if I have to hurt bad people who get in my way.

10
UNLEASHED

AVA AND I walk together, following the jumbled footsteps of the boys who navigate the faint trail. The dust from their pounding, bulky boots tickles my nose. Noticing my discomfort, she hands me a clean cloth. Her personality is effortless, just like her boyfriend Maddux. Both of them are so positive, even when the world around them seems to suck. It's amazing and I hope one day to live my life with this attitude. She might look like a fierce and towering warrior, but her spirit is nothing like that. Curiosity boils over and I find myself eager to learn more about her.

"Why were you hunting down Harvesters in the inner cities?"

"Well..." she looks up to the lush, overhanging evergreens, "it's simple, really. When you were raised by them, if that's what you call it, you can only handle so much cruelty before you turn on your own."

Her words stop me in my tracks. Catching up to her I ask, "Raised by Harvesters? How does that even happen?"

"My mother was a *pet* for one of the clans." She returns her focus to the trail. "She got pregnant and before the men discovered this she ran away, fleeing to the Vernon Trust up north."

"The Vernon Trust?" I ask.

"Yeah, this was before they became the Vernon Society."

Most of the sector groups back then were more about gaining prestige than stealing power and land. They were superficial and wanted to build little utopian societies to gain the respect of the other groups. It was like a rich boys' club, and they all needed more members to be bigger than the other clubs. This was before they started abusing Influencers. After that, it was all about greed and control.

Ava pulls her ponytail forward and plays with the shiny ends. "I was born a few months later and all seemed well until my mother's former clan discovered where she was," she says. "The Harvesters nearly wiped out the whole Trust before they found us. The Vernon Trust made a deal with them and gave us up like we meant nothing to them. My mother's Harvester master, my father, made an example of her by hanging her from a freeway overpass. I was raised by the other Harvester pets until the age of ten."

"Oh my gosh," I gasp. "That's horrible. I'm sorry. How did you ever get out of there?"

"My push ability showed up and saved the day," she says looking to the heavens above. "That's why I believe our abilities, no matter how harsh they can be, were given to us so we can make this existence better for all who are good in this world."

This makes sense now; why she is so positive even when her ability is so dark. She must believe defeating the ugly elements of this world sometimes requires the use of not-so-pretty methods.

She tells me the story of her escape. To avenge her mother's death, her biological father was put into a 'coma of fear,' as she describes it. She says he is in a loop inside his own mind replaying his darkest fears.

"Harvesters are the most fearful people in the world," she says. "Desperation, fear, and selfishness only create a reality of paranoia and hate. I will never allow myself to be afraid again."

My life became scary and depressing once I started fearing what my ability can do to people. If we truly share this conscious reality and we all shape it, then I need to do my part in making it as positive as possible. I have the power to bring more change to this world than anyone has ever seen before. No longer will I hide this ability because of fear. It's time to embrace this gift and use it to make a difference in this world.

11

HAWTHORNE

WE'VE REACHED THE outer edge of the Hawthorne hub, just outside the area where Magnus patrols. We won't make our move until it gets dark, so we have a couple of hours to rest and prepare. That two-hour hike had us going up and down hills the entire time, and now my knees are throbbing. This rest is definitely called for. We find a fallen pine tree and all take a seat side by side. Farren sits to my left and Ava finds a spot to my right. I feel like one of the "cool kids" at the shelters.

"Alright, guys, it's time to iron things out," Farren says. "We know our strategy, but we need to come up with the extraction point and figure out the diversion."

Maddux leans forward and suggests, "I can find where the hub's Influencer is located. Then Ava can move in and push the vulnerable citizens to create a little panic."

"That will work." Caiden nods in anticipation. "The rest of us will breach the settlement wing and make our way to the hub's courtyard. From there Kaylin can use her mojo to find her friend."

Mojo is not what I would really call my ability, but I understand what he is saying. It has always been easy to feel the people I have the closest bond with. Almost like I sense when our awareness intersects.

"Kaylin, are you okay with all this?" Farren asks.

"Yeah, I'm ready."

Farren and Caiden go over a crude layout of the hub and plot out a way through the settlement wing to reach the courtyard. Once you move through the checkpoint, there is a clearing that separates both structures. They mention at this spot we will need to wait for the diversion in order to find an unmanned opening to the hub. I just hope I don't slow them down.

The planning dies down as our hunger kicks in. Maddux tosses each of us a food ration. I get a salmon dinner pack. There is nothing like a fake protein and mushy rice with water. Food is food, though.

After slopping down their rations, Ava and Maddux slide off the tree to the ground, where they snuggle up together. It's been a while since I've seen anyone show affection like this. They really do like each other and it shows. I try not to stare as they tease one another. With my arms folded and head high, I act like

I'm not uncomfortable. Just then Farren slides closer to me. The universe must be toying with my nerves.

"When we get Amanda back, will you finally trust me?" he asks.

I haven't thought about his act of betrayal since he convinced me to go with him to meet the resistance. This really doesn't make sense, but I've grown to care for and need him in a way. I'm just not sure if it's an Influencer trust thing, a silly girl thing, or maybe both. Whatever it is, I need to put it away as there are much bigger things to focus on right now.

I turn to him and say, "I don't control trust, or at least I don't think I do. It just happens. Let's just not die first, okay?"

"Yeah, that sounds good," he says, smiling.

* * *

Caiden is playing with his gun. Not sure why he is so eager to jump into battle or conflict or whatever, but he keeps checking his wrist display and saying, "It's almost go time."

I take a deep breath to quiet my nerves. I catch Farren looking at me as he talks to Maddux. They look like they are discussing something serious. Curiosity and an underlying lack of trust make me approach them to see what's going on. They abruptly finish talking and break apart. That was odd. I catch up to Farren as he walks back to his pack near the fallen tree.

"What was all that sneaky talk about?" I ask.

"Sneaky talk?!" he says with a less-than-convincing grimace.

"Yeah, you and Maddux seemed to be plotting something over there."

"Oh, no…" He pauses. "Just simple strategy stuff, that's all."

I don't press him any further, but something is definitely up. To be honest, I can't really focus on this right now, as my nerves are trying to take over. An equally deep swallow follows each deep breath. I have to rein these feelings in if I'm going to be of any help on this mission. Farren notices my behavior and rests his hand on my back. His touch feels so warm and caring that it intensifies my nervous energy. He leans his head down to catch my eyes and asks, "Are you sure you're ready for this?"

"No, but I have no choice at this point, do I?"

Caiden signals to Farren that they're ready to move out. Maddux tells us to look out for Ava's diversion and then move in on the hub once we get the signal. We part ways with them and get ready to push forward.

Farren, Caiden, and I start to make our way to the west side of the hub, where the settlement wing's entrance lies. I remember this part of the hub because Farren took me there as his prisoner for processing. That's not a pleasant memory, but now it feels completely different.

Caiden has been watching the Magnus patrols for the last hour. He informs us that it should be clear now, as they have just passed the checkpoint that we need to go through. He says they will not return for about twenty minutes. This doesn't give Maddux and Ava much time to do what they need to do, but they say it shouldn't be an issue.

Farren tells me that once we get to the wall we will be out of the patrol's sightlines. From there we will wait for the signal and then take advantage of the chaos to make our way past the guards at the settlement wing's entrance. There's talk about a huge clearing inside the outer wall, and rooftop snipers. They keep relaying details of this plan to me, but I can't focus and just want to get it over with. Farren assures me this is all possible, but I am having some serious doubts now. Nevertheless, we start running from the cover of one tree to the next. Caiden lumbers along breaking branches and making all sorts of noise. Every crackle from his clunky boots sends shockwaves of fear down my spine. This is not as stealthy as I was hoping it would be. Farren, on the other hand—who is actually bigger than Caiden—is having no problem navigating the terrain quietly. If I wasn't so afraid of what is around the next turn I would be sprinting past these lugs. I guess there's one benefit to traveling miles and miles every day just to stay safe.

We burst out of the dense forest into the clearing before the hub's towering wall. Caiden's lack of an implant makes it vital that we don't let this mission linger. We don't want him exposed to the hub's Influencer. He directs us to a couple of overgrown Buckeye trees that line the wall, about twenty yards from the settlement wing's gate. We're exposed here, and I don't like it. We run as fast as we can to try to reach the cover near the wall when a distant alarm grabs our attention. We reach the trees and drop to the ground, nearly toppling over each other. Farren puts his arm over my chest and clutches my shoulder, locking me in place. Caiden has his weapon drawn and points in the direction of the gate. Staring through the trees, we collectively stop breathing.

A couple of minutes pass with only the faint sound of the alarm repeating in the background. Farren loosens his grip and relaxes his body. Caiden turns to him and whispers, "The others must have tripped an alarm. We need to decide if we're going to abort this mission or still wait for their signal."

"What is this signal we are waiting for anyway?" I whisper.

"Maddux and I have two-way radio functionality on our wrist displays," Caiden says, scanning over the clearing with intense focus.

"Two-way radio?!" I blurt. "Every sector group monitors for those things. They will hear you guys and—"

Farren cuts me off and says, "Kay, it's okay, we aren't using them for communication. Our tech guy, Owen, figured out a way to set the radio function of the device to send a simple signal in between the channels. We can't talk to each other, but we can listen for the steady signal sent from any nearby radio-enabled device. When we hear it, we will know Ava's push has taken hold."

Another five minutes pass and no signal. Doubt overtakes their faces. We need to act soon or we put our chances of escape at risk due to the increased Magnus patrols from the triggered alarm. Caiden leans upon one of the trees, his foot tapping over and over. I can tell he might explode at any moment. He is not designed to wait patiently. I sneak a glance at Farren. His brow is rigid and his eyes are locked forward. His mind must be on overdrive, thinking of every possible outcome. Seconds later, his head notches up as he breaks from his trance. He leans toward me and says, "Can you feel or sense anything? I mean… Have you ever been able to pick up on things that surround you? Both Maddux and Jax have some sort of internal Influencer sixth sense. Maybe you do, too."

Even though I'm supposed to be this powerful Influencer, I've never really thought of my ability as a daily part of my life. It was always something I've tried to hide and only use in extreme situations. Because of this, I've never tested what I can really do.

"Um, I really don't know," I say. "I get slight feelings around people, but that's about it."

It's been ten minutes now since that alarm went off and there is still no sign from the others. Even Farren is getting antsy, looking over his shoulders every few seconds. His eyes have an intensity now that makes me worry even more.

"Please, Kaylin," he begs. "You need to try to open your mind to the environment. See if you can get a better picture of what's going on. Jax told me that when Magnus makes him manipulate a large population, he always dissects the cluttered voices during the push. This allows him to use strong-minded people from the group to radiate his push out even further."

Farren tells me that when Jax does this, he can get a picture of what that person is seeing and feeling. It's not the clearest, but it's like he's piggybacking on their mind to feel reality from their point of view.

Those cluttered voices are the worst part of a push—besides the end result, of course. The confusion and chaos are overwhelming. My mind is no longer alone during this and it feels so intrusive. Now Farren wants me to invade someone else's mind. It's bad enough that I've forced people to do horrible things. Now he wants me to pry into their heads and basically spy on them?

Noticing my lack of response, Caiden pleads, "You want to save your friend, don't you? Now is not the time to fall apart on us."

Amanda has done too much for me to just give up and run away. I need to believe in what Ava said about our ability. No matter how it sometimes hurts people, the purpose of it is to make this collective existence better.

"Okay, okay. I'll try."

"Those voices during the push are just a jumble of individuals," Farren says. "Just try to hone in on one to pick up whatever you can."

Just like with any push, I extend my consciousness out to the surrounding area. The intensity of the situation is making it hard to concentrate. Interruptions are slowing my reach. I feel the expanse and then it quickly retracts. It doesn't help that Caiden and Farren are watching my every move. *Come on, Kaylin, focus.* I take a deep breath and pull my knees to my head to create my own little cocoon. This seems to help, as I feel less exposed. After a burst of flickering lights splash across my mind, I hear the muttering of random voices. Farren says to try to lock in on anything that sounds operational, whatever that means. I believe what he means is to listen in on thoughts of Magnus personnel thinking about their responsibilities. If I can get any insight into what is going on inside, we can make our decision about continuing the mission.

From all the pointless internal dialogue, I pick out thoughts about securing the east wing or gate. It's faint and sounds like someone yelling across a crowded room. Quickly I sense myself drawn closer to the presence and the words become louder. The other voices dim and turn into background chatter. Focusing on the voice, I see brief flashes of this person's thoughts. Almost like layers of video flying at me from all directions. I can hardly grab hold of them as they move on and fade so fast. I try to lock on to the voice again and just as I do, the moving thoughts slow down. It's like I can bring this person's reality to a crawl while I pick through the mind for information. These visual thoughts become windows into what this individual is experiencing at the moment. I can tell this is a guy, as I see glimpses of his arms and hands. Now, I just need to figure out if this man has any real information or not.

His current experiences are pretty dull and not very helpful. He's just watching people while rarely moving. He seems to be the typical guy, just checking out girls most of the time. I need to sort through this pointless crap and see if he knows anything of use. Everyone is depending on me to save this mission. That's when an experience he's having catches my attention.

A hazy vision shows me a young lady that comes up to him and asks, "Where do I need to be for this alert? I'm in Group C."

Now we're talking. When he's not flirting with girls, he seems to be helping people find where they need to go.

"Well, hello there," he says to her. "Just head to your assigned section at the east gate."

I'm able to reach this young man with my push so he must not have the block implant, but he still seems to work for the hub. Shortly after this, a Magnus security guard approaches him. This pudgy little guard is dressed in the typical dark outfit of this group. I never understood why these groups like to dress their so-called employees in these dreary, stiff uniforms. Already controlled by the

Magnus Influencers, there's no need to intimidate the civilians. It must be a guy thing or something.

"Hello, sir." He straightens as the Magnus guard addresses him.

"You're doing a great job, kid," says the guard. "Just stay focused on the task and not so much on the girls, please."

Whoever I'm connected to seems to be a willing sympathizer. He's eager to be a part of this group. I pick up on his desires to be implanted and promoted to an official member of Magnus. That makes no sense to me, but I don't have time to judge him right now. I have to tell the others what I've seen.

Swiftly pulled back into my individual awareness, I let go of this person's being. The voices disconnect, once again leaving me alone with my own thoughts. As the current moment takes hold, anxiety fills me once again. There's something about being in the midst of a push that clears the mind and protects me from my personal weaknesses. An airy gasp slips out as I bring myself back to my current state of reality.

Farren leans uncomfortably close to my face. "Please let me know you saw something."

I sit upright, gathering myself. "That alarm is a breach alert and they're moving everyone to the east gate as a precaution."

"This isn't as we planned it, but..." Caiden stops to think. "It means our mission is still viable."

What does that mean? I don't like the unknowns from this change of events. I grab Farren's wrist and argue, "Doesn't a breach alert mean they think someone has breached the hub? Haven't we lost our element of surprise?"

"Chaos is chaos," he replies. "We either move now or never. They'll regroup and fortify the hub once they assess the situation. This is Amanda's only chance."

There it is again, that magic word: 'Amanda.' Every time I hear her name, my motivation and courage return. I nod in agreement and wait for them to plan our next move.

Caiden doesn't waste any time before he signals to Farren that we're going to move on the settlement wing entrance. He leads with his weapon drawn as Farren trails behind me giving me a reassuring nod signaling that he has my back.

Just as they predicted, the entrance is locked down, as the guards have fallen back to make sure the main hub structure is secure. We make our way to the gate, which is no more than a large steel door flushed into the twelve-foot-tall cement wall. Barbed wire protects the top of the wall, so our only way in is through this entrance.

Caiden reaches into his pack and pulls out a small metallic disk no bigger than my palm. Quickly he places it near the door's locking mechanism. He pulls two pins from the side and steps back a few feet. I cover my ears and turn my face instinctively, but there is no explosion.

A small circle has bored through the door as white-hot, melted steel drips from its edges. With one swift kick, Caiden knocks the door open. It bellows and screeches to a stop. Farren takes cover on one side of the door as Caiden covers the other. Guided behind Farren, his weapon-free hand covers my torso as we creep closer to the opening. He pulls me in close to his body.

Caiden waves to us, signaling that we're clear to move. Farren takes my hand and leads me into the settlement wing. This building is no more than a couple of construction site offices seamed together. I have seen these portable buildings all over Lost Souls, used for homes and shops. Caiden follows us in and crouches down at the unmanned reception desk. Farren and I fall back to a row of filing cabinets that line the wall. This structure is broken into several rooms segmented by temporary walls with large plastic windows. The purpose of this wing is to assess the usefulness of new recruits who are brought into Magnus from the south entrance to this group's sector. Lined with folding chairs, the rooms almost look like small classrooms, but no one receives an education here. Recruits, thoroughly examined, find out how they best fit with Magnus' plans to utilize them for the so-called betterment of the group. The cloudy memory of Mavis Edgeley forcing me to watch Amanda sit through a settlement evaluation ignites a fire in me. I'm eager to get going now and bring her to safety.

We make our way to the rear exit. Fully evacuated, we have no trouble making our way through the settlement wing. I peek out the window and notice the large clearing from this building to the hub's main structure. Floodlights brighten every inch of the massive opening. Earlier at our little campsite, Farren mentioned the clearing is about seventy-five yards across. Looking at it now, this open space is a lot of ground to cover while avoiding detection. They take care of the vegetation really well, too. There isn't any groundcover to use when we cross.

Farren left his post with Magnus to come after me only a few days ago. Because of this, he knows more than Caiden about the current tactics of these hubs. Caiden was once a security head for a hub up north, but that was more than a year ago and things have changed. So, from this point, Farren will take the lead. Plus, Caiden is not shielded like Farren is with the implant. If the Influencer of this hub figured out we're here, Caiden would be at risk of manipulation. Looking up toward the guard posts on the top of the hub, Farren squints and says, "Those posts are never left unmanned. I can't see, but I know they're up there scanning the clearing.

"We'll split up," he decides. "Caiden, you make your way across the left side and Kaylin and I will take the right."

"Hey, Farren, don't complain about having to drag her with you when I smoke you to the other side," he grins.

"Shut up," I say, rolling my eyes.

Caiden laughs, checking his weapon. Farren takes one last glance at the clearing and says, "Let's do this."

We fly into the clearing, separating after seconds. Caiden lumbers away from us as Farren and I sprint out in front. It seems like we are running for forever, but it has only been a few seconds when we see the mammoth structure come into focus. Just as we are about to take cover at the base of the hub, we hear a blast from the roof followed by a groan from Caiden in the distance. The protruding features on the hub's walls block our view of him. A second blast screeches into the clearing. We see no sign of Caiden.

12

CHAOS

FARREN KICKS OPEN a door that leads us into a storage facility that smells of compost. The light from the clearing explodes through the entrance. Shadows cast on the back wall reveal huge, ancient-looking machines that must maintain the clearing. He has me crouch against the wall just to the side of the door. He instructs me to stay put and then without another word he leaves. Slowly, inch by inch, I stick my head out to see him following the wall, never taking his eyes off the top of the hub. With his pistol pointed at the roof, he is ready to fire. Slipping around the corner, he's gone. Caiden is out there somewhere around that bend and Farren is going to find him, dead or alive. I'm alone now with no weapon and no idea of what to do next.

Minutes pass and I'm still sitting here where Farren put me, like a dog minding its master. Running my fingers over the contours of the pendant on my necklace takes my mind off the intensity of the moment. Hope for them to return is fading. Anxious energy is trickling out of every inch of me. I can't sit here any longer just waiting for them. Sliding the necklace back under my shirt, I release a deep breath that motivates me to move. Looking over the storage area, I search for anything that might help my situation. It won't be long before Magnus sends someone down here to investigate the incident. Quickly, I find a locked door on the rear wall. There is a security panel next to the latch. Without the hub's access codes, there will be no way I can break through this door. Just as I turn to figure out what to do next, the panel on the door lights up. Someone is accessing this room from inside the hub. I stumble over the entry step, falling down while shuffling backward along the ground. A large tire attached to one of the green machines is the closest hiding spot I find. Tucked into a ball behind this massive rubber wheel, my breathing becomes fast and uncontrollably loud. A metal sounding clank bounces off the ceiling and the door creaks open. Several heavy footsteps fill the entry. A strong voice says, "We know you are in there. Throw your weapon on the ground near the door and come out with your hands on your head."

Fear stops my breathing and I nearly vomit. Should I take my chances and make a break for the door? Or should I give myself up and, like Amanda, become a prisoner of Magnus? Before I have a chance to decide, someone puts a hand over my mouth. I'm just about to claw at the hand when Farren whispers in my ear, "Don't scream, it's just me." My body relaxes as I nod and put my hand on his forearm to let him know that I understand.

"We don't have time," he whispers. "We have to run now."

Without warning, he pulls me up and we rush to the door that leads out to the clearing. Several Magnus guards shout and come after us. "Stop or we'll fire!"

Just before we get to the exit, Farren throws something behind us into the room. Guns fire and bullets zip past my head as he drags me to the ground just outside the door. A blast erupts inside the storage room, forcing warm air to rush out the entrance. The ground rattles beneath us as I find cover near Farren. We pull ourselves up to make sure we are out of the line of fire from the guards posted on the roof. There is no longer anyone rushing at us, but we are far from safe. Farren pulls me along the side of the hub until we reach a group of three large sewage lines coming out from the towering structure. Caiden lies tucked in between the rusty pipes trying to tend to his own wound. A bullet through his right leg has crippled him.

Reaching into my small backpack, I pull out the extra HypoPatch kit I salvaged from the ranger outpost. This worked wonders on the cuts on my arms, but will only stop the bleeding and relieve some of his pain. The ointment I used on my head would work great, but that was the only dose I found. Caiden removes the temporary wrap he fashioned from the sleeve of his shirt. Farren uses his small canteen to flush out the bloody bullet hole that has left an exit wound on the back side of his leg. Caiden bites his lip to hold back a groan. Once the wound is cleaned, I spray the antiseptic on both sides and then wrap the leg with the bonding film. Instantly Caiden's face relaxes as the spray manages to ease some of his pain. Now it's just a question of what we're going to do with him.

"You sure do come in handy sometimes," says Caiden.

"Sometimes, huh?" I ask, smiling.

Farren wastes no time and pulls him to his feet, supporting his weight on his shoulder. Before we start to move, Caiden stops us. "Hold on there, cowboy. I'm not going to be able to hold your hand through this mission anymore. You're going to have to leave me here and finish this thing without me like a big boy."

"That's not happening," says Farren. "I'm not leaving you here to be captured."

"Hey, m-man…" Caiden stammers in pain. "It'll be okay. I won't let them find me."

Grimacing, he sits back down between the corroded pipes. The indecision on Farren's face amplifies as he watches his friend give up. This mission is going from bad to worse and we are no closer to rescuing

Amanda. Grabbing Farren's hand, I look directly into his eyes and say, "We have to go or we are all going to die."

"Listen to your girlfriend," blurts Caiden. "You've got bigger things to do now."

Even in this intense moment, my cheeks get warm and flush with blood. I shake it off and nudge Farren to move. He promises to come back for him after this is over, no matter what it takes.

Reluctantly, Farren takes the lead and guides us along the wall as we head to the east side of the hub where all the citizens are gathering for this emergency. He refuses to look back at Caiden as we leave. I guess it's his way of not emotionally giving up on him.

We must be out of sight of the tower guards, as no one is raining bullets on our heads at the moment. That's always a good thing. Farren knows the ins and outs of these hubs, so he understands where the personnel will be during every situation. This gives us a shot at finding Amanda.

So far we're able to move without notice. We only have one more bend to go around before we reach the east side of the hub. Just as we inch our way around the corner, we are driven back by a storm of bullets. Countless flashes burst from the roof's edge. They were expecting us. It makes sense why we were able to travel so effortlessly up to this point. We're pinned down now with nowhere to go. Clinging to the wall just behind the guard's sights, we wait hoping for a break in the fire. Their shots are meant to contain us until we give ourselves up or make a break for the main wall. I can see in Farren's eyes that he wants to edge out to fire back, but the blinding floodlights from the roof make it impossible to find a clear target. It would be great if we could take the lights out, but there are thirty to forty on each side and not enough bullets to make a difference.

With no other options, he tells me he's going to lay down some cover fire and commands me to sprint back to the settlement wing building. This is not a plan at all; it's a death sentence for both of us, but we have no other options. I'm about to charge into the opening when he grabs my shoulder and says, "Wait."

He looks at me as if he has found the answer and says, "I know this is hard for you, but can you try to use your push to get some animal backup? It's all we've got right now."

Using my push to turn animals into my personal killing machines is not something I ever wanted to do again. But, after talking to Ava about doing whatever is needed, I'm not quite as reluctant. Even with my heightened state of anxiety, I'm sure I could push past it, but while looking out at the clearing I realize it would be pointless. Those twelve-foot walls would prevent any would-be assassins from the wilderness from reaching us. Even if they somehow managed to get over, there is no way they would be able to scale the sides of the enormous hub to reach the gunmen.

Before I have a chance to talk to Farren about what I've realized, a sudden cascade of loud clicks rushes through the rooftop. Within seconds, the clearing goes dark. All that remains from the floodlights is a cooling glow that fades around the edges. Farren moves in front of me, shielding me from whatever might come next. We remain quiet and still with our eyes shifting back and forth from the clearing to the roof. I have no idea what just happened. We can't see more than ten feet in any direction. Farren leans in and says, "We need to move now before they turn them back on."

He grabs my wrist and pulls me around the bend where we were pinned just moments earlier. We nearly scrape our shoulders as we follow the rough wall on our way to the east entrance. The pounding of my heartbeat overtakes our heavy footsteps and I feel the well-known grip of fear take over my body. I'm just about to collapse when I slam into Farren's solid back as he stops abruptly. He looks back to let me know we are here.

We stand just feet away from a set of metal doors. Farren crouches down and without notice pulls me to my knees. His gentle touch from before has changed to a rough grasp of urgency now. I understand, but I still don't like it. My nerves have settled some, but we are again stuck leaning up on the hub's wall trying to figure out what to do next. A subtle buzzing on Farren's wrist display startles me. It's the signal from Maddux that we were waiting for earlier. They must be alright, but this signal was supposed to let us know it was okay to move from the settlement wing to the main structure.

"What does this mean?" I ask.

"I'm not sure, but at least they're okay," he says. "It must have been them that cut the power, though."

"At least they're okay," I say while exhaling. "What are we supposed to do now?"

Locked from the inside, the solid metal doors prevent us from moving forward. Farren points out the metal shielding surrounding the locking mechanism, so even shooting at it with his gun would not get us anywhere. I didn't really want to let the whole hub know we're out here by firing guns off anyway. I realize that it's time to do my part and find Amanda. Standing now, I turn to Farren, who is still crouched against the wall near the doors.

"I'm going to find Amanda now. When I do, I'll push her to find an exit."

"Are you sure?" Farren asks. He takes my hand.

"Well, one of us needs to do something, and that cute little gun of yours is useless. I owe this to Amanda." I catch him smirking as he rolls his eyes at me.

The borrowed mind of that Magnus volunteer revealed that all civilians were being directed to the east wing of the hub during the breach alert. Amanda should be somewhere nearby. I just need to find her familiar awareness and use her fear of Magnus to motivate her to escape. She will forgive my meddling in her head if I get her out of here.

Amanda's mind is very familiar to me. The few times I have dug into her consciousness, I've sensed only honesty. Filled with hate for the ones who have done her wrong, but overflowing with love for me and the memories of her family. Her feelings have always teetered on the edge. This explains her deep desire to care for me as well as her instant mistrust of anyone associated with sector groups.

It almost seems easy to open my mind for this push, as there are so many souls nearby ready to be shaped. Unlike other Influencers, I'm able to quickly grab onto the surrounding consciousness. The collective energy of a large group like this feels warm to me. My stomach radiates the heat, quickly filling my chest and moving on throughout my whole body. I've never used my ability on this many people before. It's like being connected to something much bigger than me. Never before has using my push been anything other than horrifying, but this time is different. I'm doing this for the good of the people being influenced instead of causing them pain.

The push pulls the hub's citizens into my mind, flooding me with the thoughts and inner voices of hundreds of people. They are overwhelmed and scared. Flashes of their recent thoughts burst before me. Glimpses of people confused about what is going on. Some who are searching for loved ones and more just rushing to find a safe place to be. Just as I begin my search for Amanda, I come across a sensation that I have never felt before. I'm losing people. Voices disappear and thoughts fade out. Plucked right out of my push is the best way to describe what is going on.

It takes me a few seconds before I realize what is happening. The hub's Influencer must have felt a shift in the crowd and has begun trying to tame the group. My control is faltering. I need to act fast or this mission will become a failure. While trying to refocus, I remember what Farren said about how Jax uses people in the push as amplifiers to expand his reach. Jax would somehow search out the most consciously aware in the group and piggyback on their minds to extend the push. The question is how.

With my push on the verge of collapsing, I hunt for people who in some way feel different from the rest. Not knowing exactly what to look for, I comb over the clutter of minds in the area. Most people's awareness seems to revolve around their physical being. It's like they stick to their own personal bubble that limits their connections to reality. Once I identify this pattern, I start to find greater waves of consciousness that radiate from certain individuals. In this state, these people's awareness overlaps and pours over the rest. It's like watching larger drops of rain among smaller pounding in a puddle. Their ripples spread out over the water and overtake the smaller ripples. Soon, all I see are the large drops. I mentally grab hold of these people's awareness, and soon I find my push envelop the collective consciousness. These minds strengthen my bond with the group. Influencing them is easier, as they're willing to be part of something bigger than themselves. Within a few moments, I overtake the crowd and force out the other Influencer. I now control the group's complete awareness.

This feels amazing to do for the first time. I've never known this sensation before. Easily overriding this hub's Influencer gives me a sense of satisfaction. Maddux was right: Each Influencer has to uncover their potential and to do that a push has to be soaked in the reality of the moment. No training can prepare me for what I am becoming.

Amanda stands out among all the citizens. I recognize her thoughts, as most of them include me. Her presence is strong and the hate for Magnus easily consumes her foremost awareness. Her consciousness ripple is easily the largest in the group. It makes perfect sense why it would be, as she has been stuck with me for the past eight years. Living with an Influencer for that long has to rub off on you. She is pretty open to my thoughts on reality and knows everyone is part of something bigger than their own little world.

Feeling Amanda's presence reminds me how much I miss and need her. This familiar feeling is comforting. It's time to get her back. I narrow in and start pushing the idea of fleeing upon her. I project an urgency to move and find a way out. Pulling her memory of when I first used my push on those bullies at our shelter gives her that need to move. Her mood becomes unsteady and stress fills her mind. With the bond created by my push, I relive this with her and my own experience of that day filters into her awareness, only increasing her desire to find safety. I create a sense of warmth and security near the back side of the large area where this group is corralled. Using the memories of her parents, I radiate a familiar mood that guides her in the right direction. I tap into her current thoughts and see she is nearing an empty corridor lit only by soft red lighting that must be powered by an emergency generator.

This new visual sensation I'm tapping into today is crazy. Feeling people is one thing, but watching their experiences is odd.

A flash shows me several similar metal doors lining the cool, dark hall. Then I notice a door that stands out among the rest. It resembles a hatch that I recall from when I was held here a few days ago. A pulsing green light bulb hangs above it, casting an eerie glow over the door. Maddux told me to look out for these hatches because they always led outside into the clearing. The only problem now is that she has to somehow open this locked exit.

Thrust out of my push, I snap back to reality to find Farren dragging me to a pillar just past the east gate.

"What the hell are you doing?" I shout. "I had her. She's stuck at a locked exit."

"Calm down," he whispers, muffling my mouth with his hand. "They know we're out here. I heard someone coming from the hub. They're just around this corner."

My throat drops as we hear shuffling footsteps just yards away. Farren signals that he's going to let them come to us and then take them out. Grabbing the barrel of his gun, he prepares to disable them without firing the weapon. We don't want to alert others of our location by shooting up the place.

The pace of the footsteps increases and become louder. The beating of my heart intensifies as Farren shuffles closer to the edge of the wall. He raises his arm to strike when I pick up on a familiar presence. I lunge at Farren's arm and pin it to the wall. He glares at me, confused. Before I have a chance to explain, Amanda stumbles around the corner and screams as she nearly runs into us.

"Amanda, Amanda, Amanda," I quickly blurt while grabbing her arms to steady her frantic body.

Her eyes meet mine and in an instant, her panic turns to joy. A huge smile fills her face. I release my grip on Farren's wrist to embrace Amanda. Her legs collapse and we buckle to the ground. She squeezes me extra hard, making sure this moment is real.

"I knew it was you," she insists. "I knew you would come back for me."

Pulling back, she puts both hands on my face while taking a deep breath. Without thinking, she glances up at Farren who is standing ready to attack whatever comes next. Surprised, she wrestles me away from him and snarls, "What the hell is this? What is he doing here? What's going on?"

"Calm down. It's okay," I explain. "It's a long story, but he came with me to rescue you."

"Please, Amanda, settle down," Farren pleads. "We need to get you guys out of here. We don't have time to get into this right now."

Amanda jumps to her feet. "Don't tell me to settle down," she rages.

I stand and wedge myself between them. Clutching Amanda's arms, I am able to inch her back a step. "Amanda, listen to me. I'm still alive because of him. He's on our side. We need to stop this now and get out of here before the real enemies find us. We'll talk about this when we're safe."

Not having any other options, she nods in agreement. I grab her hand as Farren leads us back along the hub's wall toward the drainage pipes where Caiden is holed up. I can tell Farren is worried about him. He grabs my free arm and nearly drags both of us away from the east gate and toward his injured friend.

As we make our way along the wall, I hear Amanda groan in pain. I turn to her and realize I am squeezing her hand way too tightly. I loosen up and give her a soft smile that she returns. Losing her was the hardest thing I've lived through. I don't want to do it again.

Dragging Amanda along, we reach the corner that marks our destination. Just beyond, I hope to find Caiden tucked between the cover of the drainage pipes. Sprinting around the wall, I crash into something that knocks me several feet to the ground. A stinging burn radiates through my chest. I look up to find Farren and Amanda slammed back by several Magnus security personnel. The burning heat of the men's 'shock sticks,' as I like to call them, stiffens their bodies as well and they fall to the ground like frozen statues. The intense pain only lasts a few seconds, but it is not something I ever want to feel again. Once the pain goes, I'm left with a tingling sensation that pricks at my limbs as I regain movement. Before we have a chance to recover, the men are standing over us pointing those fun wands in our faces. One of the men now holds Farren's recovered gun in his other hand.

Out of the shadows, I hear a familiar voice. "Welcome home, my dear."

Mavis Edgeley emerges from behind the guards and steps into the moonlight. His presence brings my thoughts back to being drugged and questioned in his office. Something about that smug voice boils my blood. I'm just about to lunge at him when Farren pulls himself up to his knees. The men prepare to stun him again when Mavis puts his boney hands on their shoulders to stop them.

"Hold on, gentlemen." Mavis adjusts his stiff suit jacket. "This is our very own Farren Knox. Have a little respect. You must be eager to explain yourself, Mr. Knox."

Farren leans one hand up against the hub's wall to steady himself. Our bodies are still weak from the electric shock. Brushing his overgrown locks from his eyes, he looks up at Mavis. "There is nothing to explain. I just wanted to give you and your men the chance to put your weapons down and surrender."

Mavis quickly shifts his attention back and forth between the guards before he bursts into laughter. It reminds me of an old drunk lady's cackle. The out-of-control, high-pitched cadence pierces my eardrums. If he didn't have that block implant, I would manipulate his little mind and make him suffer. He's the perfect example of what it means to be a Magnus official: arrogant, heartless, and corrupt.

"Oh Farren…" He pauses. "You truly are one of a kind. It's going to be such a loss for our organization. Your talents will be missed, and I just love your misguided confidence."

Mavis steps back to give the guards some room. "Keep the Influencer alive and kill the other two. The other girl has lost her welcome here at Hawthorne."

I look to Amanda and see her terror. Without hesitation, I thrust my body over her to protect whatever is to come. Turning to Farren, I notice an amused smile on his face. This isn't the best way to deal with death. There's no time to figure him out anymore. I set my attention on Amanda, her face desperate, and say, "They'll have to go through me first."

We embrace and close our eyes, making peace with our situation. I hear the guards draw their pistols and chamber their rounds. I feel Farren place a hand on my forearm. The grip is soft and doesn't feel tense at all. I hold Amanda tighter when out in the distance I hear an unfamiliar electrical sound build up and then release. There is a quick, zip-sounding discharge. Within seconds, I feel the new awareness of Farren, Mavis, and the four guards. How can this be? They all have the block implants. I open my eyes to find Farren trained on me. He gives me a reassuring nod. Confused, I turn to see the Magnus men gripping their heads in agony. Tears overflow from Mavis's eyes. His sobbing sounds like a twelve-year-old girl. I almost feel sorry for him, but then I remember who he is and what he has done.

Out of the distance, we hear someone shout, "What took you fools so long to get here?"

Farren grins and rises to his feet, pulling Amanda and I with him. He breaks away from us and nonchalantly makes his way through the Magnus men, who seem to have gone insane. He meets up with Caiden, who is propped up against Maddux. The tightness in my chest eases as I realize the rest of our team has made it back okay. Then it all starts to make sense as I see Ava walk up last. She struts up like a goddess. Those long legs just won't quit. She is somehow using her push ability to paralyze the men in their own minds. I don't understand how it's possible she can do this with them all having the implants. Ava comes up to me and gives me a big hug. Her long arms swallow me.

I look up at her and say, "How is this possible? Is this you?"

Maddux overhears me. "You can thank Owen for that. It's his latest invention. He calls it a Burst Disrupter, but I like to call it a Block Buster. It's quite brilliant. It emits an electromagnetic pulse that temporarily disables the block implants of those in close range. Pretty cool, huh?"

Our reunion is cut short as Mavis squeals like a cornered dog and takes off toward the hub. Spooked by his movements, the paranoid guards instinctively react and flee in all directions. Caiden quickly draws his gun and points it at Mavis as he runs like a chicken with his head cut off. Farren grabs Caiden's arm while stepping in front of him. They lock eyes and Farren snarls, "Hey! Think, Caiden, think! Everyone in this hub will hear that and come pouring out of every nook of this place. I'm not ready to die, are you?"

"Who the hell are these people and what is going on here?" Amanda blurts out, clearly confused.

"Guys, we need to move out now," Farren interrupts. "There will be plenty of time for Q and A once we are far from this hub. They will be looking for Mavis and when they find him, everyone and their mother will be after us. We need to take advantage of this now."

Even Amanda knows he is right as she stares at him for a second and gives him a cautious nod. Just like her, I have so many questions. Like, where were Maddux and Ava during this whole mission? And why didn't we use this "block buster" tech earlier? More questions race through my mind as we run across the dark clearing, but they will have to wait until we get far from the crippled and enraged Hawthorne hub.

13

CATCHING UP

ESCAPING HAWTHORNE WAS easy enough. All the work we did to get in made getting out a breeze. Off in the distance, we hear the disjointed ramblings of the hub's personnel scrambling to regain control of their powerless fortress. We're gone before they know what hit them. Stalks of fern are swept across our tracks, disguising our footsteps as we head back through the thick forest toward the Walton hub to regroup. Needing to catch my breath, I allow myself to relax for a moment to look over this odd pairing of freaks and castoffs. The cool glint from the moon casts just enough light to study everyone. I have never been part of a group of any kind. This feeling is so new to me. Not bad, just new.

I look over to Ava, who doesn't appear to have a care in the world. She plays with her hair while she effortlessly navigates the overgrown trail. Her ability, along with that burst tech, saved us. I would love to be there to see Mavis's pathetic face when their Influencer snaps him from the mental prison she put him in. The thought of him flipping out with rage puts a smile on my face. Then there's Maddux and Farren, who each have one of Caiden's arms draped over their shoulders. He grunts at every tree they brush up against, staring at Farren as if he did it on purpose.

On the verge of exploding, Amanda lags a few steps behind me. Not one to keep her thoughts to herself for too long, she catches up to me. "Alright, what is this, Kay? How is Farren a good guy all of a sudden? And what's with the comic book characters?" She points at the rest of the team.

When you really look at the group she has a point. Ava and Maddux look like they could be from some futuristic tribe of stunning people. Laced with tattoos they seem mysterious, even a little unrealistic. Then Caiden, with his buzzed, bright-red hair and stiff military outfit, gives you a feeling of a past you were not part of. The only one who seems to fit our current reality is Farren. "Heeellllooo, Kay?" Amanda sings, snapping her fingers in my face.

"Yeah, right... Uh, sorry." I break from my lock on Farren. "You need to relax; I promise you, we're safe."

I proceed to tell her all about how Farren got caught up in his desperate plan to save his family and how Amanda and I became a part of it. Even though he saved us both from Magnus, I can still see Amanda isn't going to forgive him that easily. She knows it was his fault we were caught in the first place. Even risking his life several times to help us doesn't break down the wall she put up to protect us. We lag behind the group to give her a chance to breathe as I continue filling her in.

"There are bigger things going on here," I say. "Farren and the rest of them are part of a pretty big resistance against Magnus. We're trying to end their hostile grip on this sector."

"We?" Her eyes almost explode from her head. "What do you mean, 'we'?"

"Um, yeah, I'm part of this now."

"You're part of this? Kaylin, we haven't gone to so much trouble to keep your ability hidden all this time just to expose it now."

I put my arm around her slight figure and pull her close. "I love you, but I'm done hiding," I say. "Hiding is not living, and it's time to use my ability for something important. I have a chance to help a lot of people and I'm not going to run from that."

A look of defeat washes over Amanda's tired face as she realizes there is no changing my mind. Or maybe she's just too exhausted to argue. She doesn't have to say anything; I know exactly what's running through her mind. That life of being scared, little kids on the run is over. Amanda will never leave my side, so supporting me is all there is now. She gives me a squeeze and rests her head on my shoulder as we catch up to the rest of the group.

We walk through the dim-lit forest, stumbling over rocks and twigs as we make our way through the faint trail. Keeping pace with the others is not that difficult, as we are stopping every ten minutes for Caiden. He's in need of medical treatment and the pain from his leg is slowing down the group. Just as we stop for our latest rest, Farren decides to join Amanda and me as we sit on a patch of dry moss lining the path. Amanda doesn't even look at him. He sits next to me and the warmth of his body radiates out and tickles my exposed arms. Lugging Caiden this whole time must be tiring. He takes a deep breath and turns to Amanda. "I'm sorry for what I put you through. I was stupid and desperate. I promise you, Amanda, I will never allow anyone to hurt you guys again. And you don't have to trust me, because I'm going to do it no matter what you think of me."

Amanda looks up at Farren with just her eyes. Not really wanting to address him, she quietly says, "Kay trusts you now and I trust her, so I guess that makes us friends—no, acquaintances. Just keep your stupid needles away from us."

A soft chuckle rattles my core as I place a hand on each of their knees. Quickly realizing what I'm doing, I pull my hand back from Farren and casually tousle my hair. He notices and gives me a smile.

"Stop playing house over there, Ferret," Caiden moans. "It's time to get to Walton."

I return a smile of my own to Farren as we get back on our feet and continue on.

Two hours later, we reach the opening that leads to the resistance-occupied Walton hub. It's two in the morning now and we are all beyond tired. We funnel through the side hatch, eventually all breaking into separate groups. Ava and Maddux find a room toward the exit. Ava told me Maddux doesn't like to be too far from an exit. Something about not liking to be in one place for too long. Farren takes Caiden to the makeshift medic's room, which is no more than a bed and a storage locker of stolen medical supplies from the Magnus Order. I ask him if he needs an untrained, clueless nurse, but he just laughs and jokes about Caiden not wanting anyone to see him cry as he gets treatment. I tell him goodnight and Amanda and I make our way to the same room I stayed in last night. We share the one bed in the room. It feels normal to have Amanda back, even if everything in our lives has changed so dramatically from just a few days prior. We lie on our backs facing the room's hatch door. Staring at the soft glowing light that hangs above the exit, my curiosity is aroused and I remember something about our rescue of Amanda.

I roll over to my side and make out the dim shape of Amanda in the darkness. "When I was using my push at the Hawthorne hub, I saw you stuck behind a security latch. Then moments later you ran into us outside. How did you get out?"

"You're not the only one who's made new friends," she says while staring up at the cracked cement ceiling. "I'm not completely helpless when you're not around."

As I have grown over the years, the relationship between us has changed. I love seeing Amanda step outside her comfort zone. Like her, I've found my own identity and become much more decisive. Less and less have I needed her guidance.

"What new friends?" I ask. "Who helped you?"

"Well, there was a cute security guard who thought he had a chance with me," she boasts. "I played him along for a day just to get close enough to find his passcode to the exit hatches. I feel kind of bad for him. He risked everything to sneak around with me."

"A boy, huh?" I say. "So unlike you, Amanda."

"Shut up!"

"I'm just saying," a childish grin stretches across my face, "I've known you for eight years now and you've never let anyone get close to you."

"That's probably because I'm too busy keeping you safe," she says. "I'm done with this chat. Let's get some sleep, please."

She rolls over and faces the wall. It doesn't take long before we are both fast asleep.

***

DAVID R. BERNSTEIN

An echoing whack on the hatch door bounces off the walls in our room. I nearly fall off the bed. Amanda cringes and pulls the covers over her head. Dazed, I drag my legs off the bed and say, "We're awake! What is it?"

A frantic Maddux commands, "We need everyone to the mess hall, now."

Grabbing a fresh outfit from the lost-and-found bag, I quickly dress. A white fitted tank and cargo pants are today's ensemble. I help Amanda find something that fits her. Half awake, she throws on a pair of dark jeans and a green, flowy top. We toss our hair into quick ponytails and bolt out the door. Although Amanda was a prisoner of Magnus, she at least was able to shower and it shows. Her hair looks to be washed and brushed. One of these days, I might be able to get a hairbrush and a shower. I would even accept a cold one at this point.

We enter the cramped mess hall only to find we're the last ones to arrive. Caiden sits at the small table. His leg is bandaged in a flexible, graphene wrap. Maddux sits next to him tugging at it as if it's a new toy. The black, carbon material firmly grips his leg, but allows for full movement. Caiden doesn't seem to be in any pain so I guess Farren knew what he was doing. Ava leans up against the rear wall snacking on a protein bar. She glances at me, giving me a sweet smile. I smile back and then turn my attention to Farren, who has his arms folded while he leans up against the food-prep counter.

He doesn't offer me his normal inviting smile, so something must be wrong.

"Sorry we didn't get here any sooner," I say while guiding Amanda reluctantly into the room. "What's going on, guys?"

Farren straightens. "I've been trying to contact Jax for the last few hours with no luck. We have to assume he has been compromised."

Amanda looks up at me and whispers, "Who's Jax?"

I shrug her off, about to ask Farren for more details, when Maddux jumps in. "It must have been our mission last night. I bet we triggered an internal investigation related to our resistance."

"Could be," says Farren. "Jax has never taken more than an hour to respond. If he's compromised, we need to move up our plans before we lose all our embedded assets. Caiden and I have already communicated with our other contact points in the nearby hubs and camps. We are having everyone fall back to this hub to regroup. We are going to move out in a few hours and take out Talas."

Move out? Take out Talas? This is happening much faster than I thought it would. I am not ready for this. I don't even know the full plan yet. I just got Amanda back and now we're about to put our lives at risk for this young and unproven resistance.

14

FEAST OR FARREN

BACK IN OUR makeshift quarters, Amanda and I sit on the edge of the thin mattress. We're supposed to regroup in the mess hall at nine a.m. That gives me an hour to bring her up to speed about Jax and the resistance. Before I have a chance to say anything, Amanda blurts out, "Okay, you've had your fun. Can we get out of here now?"

"As tempting as that sounds right now, I've made a commitment to Farren and this resistance and I'm not giving up on all those Magnus-controlled civilians. I'm not afraid anymore, Amanda. I can't be afraid anymore."

"I know, I know," Amanda insists. "A girl can try, though."

For the next forty-five minutes, I go over the inner workings of the resistance and its leader, Jax Riley.

Amanda is more about passion than details, so I try to focus on the stories and emotions of the leadership rather than the logistics. I fill her in on how Jax and Farren are working against Magnus from the inside and how this resistance has been building for quite a while now. As I catch her up on the people I've met in the last couple of days, she seems as fascinated with Ava as I am. I'm probably making her sound like some sort of mystical goddess as I vividly describe her. Amanda can sense I have a fondness for Ava and I get the impression she is a little bit jealous of this. I reassure her no one can replace my special Lost Souls sister. Amanda is the only family I have ever known and that bond is unbreakable.

We put a change of clothes into a couple of small backpacks that Caiden gave us and head back to the mess hall. Without warning, time appears to slow as we walk down the corridor. My push ability somehow activates on its own. Through the familiar flickers of light, I see large groups of people hiking through the forest. My vantage point is several hundred yards off the ground. The sensation fills my body with adrenaline. I realize I must be recalling the recent memories of a bird soaring through the sky. The gust of wind racing past me drowns out all the chaos of the world and it feels isolated and calming. The feeling doesn't last, as I'm quickly drawn down to the earth. Thrust from soul to soul, I bounce between the focal points of the oncoming group. The Influencers and consciously free civilians that are approaching must have triggered my connection. I have not been around this many people who are aware of the reality of our existence. It's almost like I've slipped into their collective consciousness. These people are not restricted by the limitations of individual realities. It feels like lying on a beach and suddenly the tide rises, gently pulling me into a warm ocean of unity. A few seconds later the group's thoughts are sucked from my vision and within an instant, I'm brought back to the corridor.

Amanda is staring at me. "So, where did you go?"

After I explain what happened, she looks at me as if she's trying to dissect my facial expressions. More than anyone in my life, she's always known when something was happening to me. Worrying about me is just part of her makeup.

"Animals?!" her voice elevates. "Wow, that's crazy."

"Yeah, lots of things are happening now," I say. "My ability is a little more powerful than we thought."

"I'm sorry I wasn't there for you when this happened."

Purposely, I avoid too much detail, but I let her know about my escape from the ranger post. This push is tougher to accept. I don't like talking about it.

"Let's get going, okay?" I ask, hoping to avoid more questions.

Amanda knows when I'm overwhelmed. She drops the conversation—for now, at least.

After regrouping at the mess hall, we all head out to the clearing to wait for the remaining resistance to arrive. I let the guys know what I saw while in my push. Farren says based on the visions I had this particular group is no more than thirty minutes away. This gives plenty of time for Caiden to push Amanda's buttons. Leaning against the hub's outer wall, I sit back and enjoy the show.

"So you're Kaylin's mom, huh?" Caiden smirks.

"And you must be Farren's grandpa?" she replies.

He laughs. "Well played."

I watch them tease one another like siblings for a few minutes before my attention is drawn to Farren strutting toward me. I can't help notice his tall and athletic frame as he approaches. Straightening up, I brush my hair behind my ears. With a loud thud his back slams against the wall next to me. With Amanda distracted by Caiden, it gives us a moment to talk. He places his hand on my knee and asks, "Are you sure you're ready for this?" The gesture floods goose bumps down my legs and arms. I hope he doesn't notice them.

"I am ready for something new in my life," I reply. "Something that's better. Something that's different from the fear and wandering of the past six years, you know?"

"I know exactly what you mean. Ever since I was sixteen, I've been trapped in this life. A life I didn't choose. A lonely life."

I look up at him and our eyes lock for a moment before my shyness pulls me back down again.

He notices Amanda returning and pulls his hand from my knee. He leans in and whispers, "I don't want to be alone anymore."

Before I have a chance to react to this intense statement, Amanda shouts, "Hey, Ferret, don't you have some war planning to do or something?"

He rolls his eyes at Amanda's use of the nickname Caiden has given him. Even in the short time he has known her, it's clear it will be well used. Amanda sits down just as Farren gets up. I'm left with a lump in my throat as he walks off. He turns and says, "I better get ready before the groups arrive."

Quickly, I snap my head toward Amanda. "Give him a break already, will you?"

"Kay, you've known him for three days. I'm supporting you and this suicide mission, but I don't have to play nice with him to do that."

I shift my body toward her, grabbing her forearm. She's caught off guard as I lean in and say, "I am not that nine-year-old girl anymore. I don't need you protecting me. If you haven't noticed, our lives are changing. You're going to have to accept that."

"I see how you look at him," she says. "This is not just about you growing. This is about you liking this guy."

I let go of her arm and lean back against the rigid wall. Oh, man. Is she right? The accusation repeats in my head. You like this guy. Almost as if I'm responding to both of us, I say, "Maybe I do."

15

MOVING FORWARD

IT'S GETTING CROWDED here. Most of the resistance found their way to the Walton hub; the clearing is not so clear anymore. People have broken off into several groups and the leadership is scattered among them.

Maddux works with a group of Influencers they plan to use on the front lines. I heard them talking about mixing civilian fighters with these Influencers. Their push ability will counter the effect of the Magnus Influencers targeting the implant-free resistance members.

Over on the west side of the hub, near the perimeter gate, Caiden is assigning guns to fighters who have weapons training. They have been stockpiling weapons and storing them at one of the camps for the past few months. Some of the guns look pretty advanced.

I have never seen most of this stuff before. Amanda has been hanging out with Caiden for the last couple of hours. Their personalities really blend well together. She seems happy around him. It's much better than having her on my case at all times.

A gentle tap on my shoulder breaks me free from my daze. I turn to see Farren standing with two people I have never seen before. A curly-haired young guy removes a greasy glove and reaches out his hand. "Hi, I'm Owen Helix. It's nice to finally meet you, Kaylin."

I smile and shake his hand, noticing he has some sort of metal mask resting on top of his head. I recall that he's the technical wizard everyone's been talking about.

He catches me analyzing his outfit and politely says, "Sorry for presenting myself in such a disheveled manner. I've been working on vehicles ever since arriving."

The way he carries himself reminds me of the Terrance Party orphans from our last shelter. He stands tall and attentive, as if he was trained to be regal or something. Amanda's worked hard to change the way she was around everyone. She knew it wasn't an advantage to come from this former, privileged sector group. It didn't make much of a difference in the end, though.

Probably sounding like an excited fangirl I say to Owen, "Don't worry about it. Hey, you made that implant burst thing, right? It's pretty cool. It really saved our lives."

"Oh, it's always nice to meet someone who appreciates my work. That piece of tech originated from the old EMP devices the US military used in the past. Scaling down the output and focusing it on certain electromagnetic fields allowed me to fine-tune the precision to target the small implants. We don't want to fry the brains of any innocent people who might be near the burst."

Thanks to Amanda reading me every book she could find, I have become an overly curious person when it comes to new things. It's been my one true education. The shelters never cared too much about schooling, so I am grateful for the knowledge and time she has spent with me.

Before I'm given a chance to ask him more questions, Farren steps in. "Kay, I would like you to meet Miya Hurley, our embedded Magnus personnel coordinator. She worked closely with the Magnus leadership over the last few years. She knows the ins and outs of Talas."

"Well, I'm not so embedded anymore," she says in a raspy voice.

She holds out her hand and I notice her slight frame. She has a black, pixie-cut hairstyle, but more noticeable is her short stature. She barely reaches my shoulders and she can't weigh more than eighty pounds. I carefully clasp her delicate hand and shake it like I would a small child. How such a small female gained such a powerful position in the male-dominated Magnus Order intrigues me.

"So, young lady, tell me how you like our little resistance so far?" she says, as if she is much older than me. Like most in this resistance, she is young, most likely in her mid-twenties.

"Um, I like it just fine, I guess," I stammer. "I'm pretty impressed by the size of the gathering here. I didn't think the group was this big."

Together we scan the clearing before she turns to me. "Seventy-five strong and willing souls all ready to take down corruption."

Farren stands with his arms locked behind his back as he listens to her speak. His formal stance tells me he must respect this woman. They have been stationed together at the Talas hub for a couple of years now. I might be jealous of this, but I can tell he looks at her as a mentor more than anything else.

"So what made you guys join this resistance?" I say while looking at both Owen and Miya.

"Same reason you did," Owen jumps in. "Farren. He's quite the recruiter for Jax and the resistance. I would gladly give my life for this man."

"What about you?" I say, turning back to Miya. "Did Farren inspire you, too?"

"He's really grown as a leader," she says. "When he was first recruited to Magnus, he was quite immature and a little angry. Age and structure have really helped him. I am glad I was a part of that growth. I never had the connections to break away from Magnus until Farren opened up to me about Jax and the others. I am very proud to be part of this resistance. And I am even more excited to see what you are capable of. I've been hearing about the elusive Kaylin from Lost Souls for years now. The leadership of Magnus put a lot of effort into finding you. With very little luck, might I add."

It still surprises me that my one push, when I was eleven created such a recruiting frenzy. Amanda was right to keep me hidden and on the run all these years. She couldn't keep me from being recruited forever, though. The resistance has me now and I'm okay with that.

Farren tells the others that we will meet up with them later. Together we decide to take a walk around the clearing. It gives him the chance to check on the progress of the group while spending some time with me. His movements are less confident. I find myself leading this little walk as he follows in a state of disconnect. At first he is quiet, but once we create some distance from the bustle of the resistance, he opens up to me.

"Miya told me she hasn't seen Jax since he left to meet us here the other day," he says. "I'm really worried that Magnus has him now. I don't know how I'm going to do this without him."

His words are soft and missing that commanding presence I'm used to. He and Jax are the reasons for all of this progress. To lose him right before we make our move must be hard.

"He really means a lot to you, doesn't he?" I say.

"I wouldn't be doing this if it wasn't for him."

Without even thinking, I slide my fingers against his palm, taking hold of his hand. Before I have a chance to realize what I've done, he gently closes his hand around mine.

We walk like this for several moments, saying nothing, but it isn't long before we're snapped back to reality. Maddux and Ava rush up to Farren, reporting that all the groups have arrived and we need to begin our final preparations. Just as Maddux tugs at Farren, Ava pulls me away, explaining that she needs to go over the push tactics for our strike. Not ready to leave this moment, I turn to him and say, "We'll continue this later, I promise."

Maddux and Farren make their way back to the hub to plan with the leadership. Ava and I head back down to the perimeter trail to meet up with other tactical Influencers. Out of the corner of my eye, I can see that she's smiling at me.

"What are you looking at?" I ask.

She laughs and then says, "Oh, nothing, nothing at all."

This sort of attention is not comfortable at all for me. I need to stay focused on what's to come. We are preparing to take on a deadly sector group in a few hours. Who knows if I'll even be alive tomorrow.

Following Ava's lead, we stumble through a creaky metal gate, which brings us to the rear of the enormous hub. We find ourselves in a small fenced area with dried-up, raised garden beds and a few busted-up animal shelters resting against the chain-link fencing.

I don't remember seeing this part of the hub when Jax and I walked the clearing the other day. I was caught up in what he was saying, so it doesn't surprise me.

In the middle of this enclosure, five kids are laughing and playing around at a wooden picnic table. Most of them look a few years younger than me. Ava tells me these are the tactical Influencers who, like me, will be using their ability from a distance. Remembering my own experiences at Lost Souls, my throat tightens at the thought of these kids fighting for things they can't even truly understand.

Ava introduces me to the others at the gray, weathered table. She speaks of me as if I am the savior of the world. "Hey, guys, this is Kaylin. Her gifts are going to help us win this war."

She starts talking about my powerful pushes over the last few days. Hearing someone else talk about them tends to make them feel more real. This pressure put on me by Ava is not welcome, at all. I'm not as mentally strong as her yet, but I will not allow my fear to hold me back anymore. From all directions, the young Influencers begin poking and prodding me with questions.

"How are you able to control groups of people so quickly?" asks a girl who can't be much older than eleven.

Without pause, a boy at the far side of the table asks, "Can you speak to animals?"

Several more questions are fired at me. Most of them I can't answer, as I probably have less experience using my ability than they do. Still, I do my best to add to the discussion. Anything they can learn from me will help us all be better prepared for what's to come.

Ava raises one of her long legs and puts a foot on the table. The white tattoos lining her dark skin are on full display. The brittle table rattles and it gets the attention of all of us. She rests her elbows on her knee and says, "Enough gabbing, it's time to prepare for the battle."

The group falls into place, with each kid sitting at the table waiting for us to lead. I feel like one of these youths rather than a leader, but I need to be strong for them as they seem to look up to me.

"I need each of you to give Kaylin details on your push abilities," Ava says. "Let her know your strengths and weaknesses."

After a few minutes from each of them, I realize they are just, well, Influencers. Not having any specific talents other than changing the mood of a group of nearby people. Then one young boy with blond hair, no more than thirteen, catches my attention with his unique ability. His name is Trevor and his push is like nothing I have heard of before.

"I… uh…" The slender teen struggles to get the words out. "I can force my thoughts on to people from far away."

If I understand him correctly, he can project his thoughts over a large area while pinpointing who he wants to hear it. Basically, he is a mental one-way communicator.

In a soft voice, he says, "I don't change people's moods. They just hear what I think in their own head."

Fascinated, I dig deeper to learn he accesses the inner thoughts of the target and in their own voice creates a message from his mind to theirs. I bet that must freak people out. I imagine hearing my own voice in my head speaking without me actually controlling it. The tailored way some Influencers have honed their push to do certain things is crazy.

Intrigued by his ability, I step in and say, "I'm impressed, we can use this. We need you to send out our instructions as the battle evolves. Even if we can't reach the frontline Influencers, we can still react as a group much faster if we send messages to the fighters."

The boy looks up at me with wide eyes and a grin. It's a look only a mother would get when a child feels they have lived up to their parents' expectations. Most of these kids are orphans like me. Some will be fighting alongside their parents with our resistance, but Trevor is not one of them. I need to look out for him. A thirteen-year-old kid should never be asked to fight, but all of them have volunteered and we do need their help.

Finishing up the meeting, Ava instructs an eager younger girl named Envee, who has the ability to amplify another Influencer's push, to become the antenna for our group. Her nearly white hair glimmers in the sunlight. She's cute, with her delicate features and constant smile. She endlessly shifts in her seat as if needing to flee. Her eyes can't focus on one thing for too long. Licking her lips and tapping her fingers makes it look like she's hopped up on sugar at all times.

The others will strategically scan Talas' population for vulnerable civilians to mold as the attack develops. Ava and I will do what we do to create chaos in the most strategic way possible.

Returning to the clearing, we find most of the resistance has gathered near a fallen section of the hub's battered wall. Standing atop blocks of singed cement, Farren, Maddux, and Caiden prepare to address the group. Just behind them, Miya and Owen sit on a raised boulder studying the crowd. Farren notices us and waves his hand over for Ava and me to join them. Ava drags me over to the makeshift stage. Farren reaches his hand down, pulling me up effortlessly. Feeling uneasy about all the prying eyes, I find a spot next to Owen in the back. I hunch my shoulders, wishing to become invisible. Ava sits to my right and drapes her arm over my shoulders. I've never had this many people know who I am, much less, be focused on me.

A familiar awareness washes over me as I look up to see Amanda smiling at me from the back of the crowd.

She gives me a thumbs up and I read her lips. "I'm proud of you." Smiling back lifts my spirits and I feel a little better. Farren looks back and I can read it on his face. He too is making sure I'm alright. I nod to him and he turns his attention back to the crowd. I know he's taking on a bigger role since we lost contact with Jax. I can see the unease in his body. His shoulders hang lower and the way he moves is not as confident. He has to break the news to them about Jax and it won't be easy. They'll be looking to him to lead, so his words must show strength. Failing to do so could lose the trust of this young and fragile resistance.

16

MOVING OUT

FARREN STANDS AT the edge of the rebar-laced rubble, ready to lead us into a war against a powerful enemy, but first he has to win over his own army.

"We're here for one reason." Farren projects his voice over the crowd. "All of you have been affected by Magnus or one of these other corrupt sector groups. They have taken our freedom and manipulated our realities." He inches closer to the edge of the rubble platform. "The time is now to break the mental and physical hold this evil group has over our friends and families. We are taking our stand... for... um... we need uh..."

He pauses and looks at the ground. The crowd begins to look back and forth at each other, confused. I can feel the tension as they wait for him to continue.

"I'm sorry," he confesses. "I wasn't supposed to be doing this." He takes a deep breath.

"Most of you are not aware of this, but Jax Riley has been out of contact for over thirty-six hours," he continues. "We have to assume he's been compromised."

You can almost see the anxiety in the group as people shift in place, muttering to each other. I can feel the change in their mood. I am flooded with anxiety as they look to Farren for answers.

"I've always known my role in this resistance," Farren continues, "but with Jax gone, I have taken over as leader." He paces a few steps back and forth.

Farren's movements slow as he regains his composure. Just before he gathers himself to continue, a raspy male voice calls out from the back of the crowd. A bearded man who looks like he has seen better days shouts, "We can't do this without Jax. He is our leader, not you."

The murmuring of the crowd intensifies. People look around, seeking answers and guidance. Doubt fills the air.

"We need to rethink this, we are not ready," a young woman blurts out.

Shortly after, a boy no older than Trevor steps out in front of the crowd and cries out, "I don't want to do this anymore."

Similar comments intensify and begin to merge into one unified uproar of doubt. Farren has lost the group as the realization of Jax's absence has blanketed the resistance. I have only known Jax for a brief time, but I do understand his importance. The calming influence he radiates can draw you in. Even without using his push ability, he has a way of making you feel at ease. I understand how his loss can fracture this group.

"Hold on, hold on," Farren urges. "We need to stick together. We need to be one."

"I'm sorry," says the raspy-voiced man. "I'm going back to the camp, and I don't think I'm alone."

Gaps begin to form in the crowd as people break off. My gut churns as I feel Farren's anguish. We are losing our best chance at taking down Magnus.

Farren and the other leaders call to the crowd, but the sounds of the scattering group drowned out their voices. The tight formation of people in the clearing thins and spreads out in all directions.

Before I have a chance to think, I rush to my feet and stand by Farren's side. My push pours out of my being and within a few moments it floods over the crowd. Desperation and anxiety bounce from the surrounding reality ripples of each individual. Without even thinking about it, my desire to keep them here activates my push deeper into the gathering. Quickly a sense of confinement stops the group.

Jumping into the current reality of that young boy, I witness his most recent experience. He's terrified, looking in all directions for someone to go to. A deep-seated desire to retreat back to the group creates an awareness field that acts like a barrier in his mind. Pulled from the boy, I'm forced into the raspy-voiced man's reality. I recognize his position in the crowd. Then I notice he's looking right at me. A jolt of fear rips me from his mind. Gasping for air, I'm brought back to the platform. It isn't long before Amanda's deep awareness draws me back into the crowd and into her recent experiences. I see the consciousness bubble enclose her as well as the uneasy group. Its translucent mist seems to move and bend with each individual's attention. A cool sensation flows across her face from the edges of this illusion. Our shared experience creates what is needed to satisfy the push. Closing around the unshielded like a cloud, this barrier is a manifestation of the sum fear of the crowd. All people have the same primal instinct of falling back when scared that Influencers can tap into. My new loyalty to Farren and the resistance has awakened my ability.

Amanda's understanding of Influencer powers keeps her calm as she watches it all unfold. The crowd falls back into a tighter formation, all looking out toward the cloud that surrounds them. Fear overtakes all the people around her. They begin shouting for help. My natural empathy snaps my concentration. I leave Amanda's mind and return to my own. Closing my eyes, I draw the gathering into the center of my push as I inhale. My arms tingle and my heart pounds as I shout, "Stop!"

Bouncing from person to person, I see the barrier pushes outward and pops like a balloon filled with too much air. Tendrils of mist retreat into the nearby woods. Soon, all that is left is a tightly formed group of civilians looking confused. Gazing into the clearing, I see several people wandering around looking for answers. Farren turns to me and asks, "What just happened? Did you do something?"

The push did not affect Farren and the other implanted resistance members. Nor did it affect the Influencers among the crowd. Some of them turn to me with a look of disbelief. They have not witnessed my brand of rapid-fire influence. To them, it looks as if the group went crazy. One second they are leaving with the crowd and then a few moments later, everyone changes their mind. The smoky illusion everyone else witnessed never happened for them. I like to think of it as circumvented reality. They've been left out of the conscious fold of the unshielded and put on a different path only to be united when the push was completed. It can be disorienting. For a moment you feel disconnected from the world. As your being reconnects to the surrounding reality, you sense a rush of acceptance that is quite exhilarating. I can see on the faces of those blocked out of my push that some of them are experiencing this for the first time.

The civilians begin to put it all together as they turn to me with scowls. Justified anger has built up at the realization that they've been pushed into staying. Something needs to be said here or this is going to be a bigger mess than before I did my push.

I place a hand on Farren's wrist and raise my head to say, "I'm sorry this happened. It was not my intention to do this." I scratch my head as I look up at the blue, clear sky. "For those of you who don't know me, my name is Kaylin. I joined this cause because I believe in Farren. I barely know Jax."

The crowd stirs, but I still have their attention. "I realize I can do things that seem impossible," I say, forcing myself to continue despite my unease. "I am willing to give whatever power I have to this resistance."

I want to retreat to the loneliness of the back of the makeshift platform, but Farren stops me with his gentle touch on my shoulder and warm smile.

At the contact, I feel a surge of confidence as I continue. "I never want to subject anyone to the unwanted will of another as I just did to you. I am sorry for that. I'm one of you and I know we have to do this now or we'll never do it."

The crowd once again stirs with unease as they look to each other for what to do next. I might have forced them to stay, but it doesn't change the uniformed uncertainty that is rampant in their minds.

Before the crowd once again shatters, Caiden moves from the back to take Farren's side, resting a forearm on his shoulder. Then Maddux stands to my left and Ava takes his side as well. Owen and Miya stand, also joining the unified front. Together we peer over the gathering as leaders of this resistance.

Strengthened by the show of support, Farren steps forward and calls out to the crowd. "We might not have Jax, but we have each other. Our collective skills and abilities are far greater than anything Magnus has."

The murmurs of the crowd soften as they turn to hear us out. You can see it in their eyes: they are torn.

Ava moves from Farren's side and says, "We live in a world that is manipulated by fear and greed. There is no other group of people with the level of awareness we all possess. Our collective consciousness gives us a great advantage. Let's not waste that."

More and more of the crowd turns to focus in on us. Our words are reaching them.

Miya adds, "I've lived on the inside for way too long. They are fragile. One precise attack can bring them to their knees."

A voice from the crowd shouts, "Let's do this already. I'm in."

I track the voice and see Amanda making her way to the front. "We can tear down Magnus if you follow them." She winks at me as our eyes meet.

"Will you stand with us and end Magnus?" Farren asks. "Let's free our family and friends from a world they never chose. Jax wouldn't want it any other way."

Unified once more, the resistance's chants rattle the clearing. We are again one mind acting against the cruel oppressors known as Magnus.

***

After a full day of training and preparation, the resistance takes shelter in and around the Walton hub. Tents of all sizes line the clearing as fires add warmth and comfort. People settle in for the night and try to sleep, knowing what tomorrow will bring. Amanda and I feel uneasy sleeping with this many people around us. Even inside, in our makeshift quarters, the awareness of so many people is making it hard for me to fall asleep. Always knowing how to care for me, Amanda tells me stories of when she was younger and living with her parents. The hope the Terrance Party had and the knowledge that there was a time when optimism still filled people's minds gives me a sense of ease and allows me to finally fall asleep.

17

SLOW AND PAINFUL

A NEW DAY of unknown possibilities lies before me. But first, rations and foraged berries are today's breakfast. After a less than satisfying meal, everyone gathers in the clearing before we make our push to Talas. Farren and Caiden inform the resistance of the final details of our day. The leadership, which I guess I am part of now, ushers the march into the forest. With a half-day hike ahead of us, we need to make good time to reach Talas. The three stolen Magnus vehicles will scout out ahead to make sure the road is clear. Once again, Amanda is by my side as we take one last journey together doing whatever it takes to make a better future for ourselves. The only thing that is different is that we'll be helping far more people if we succeed.

***

A couple of hours in, and already my feet and knees are killing me. Amanda and I are used to the flat and straight old highway systems. Those endless stretches of road were easy for us. This is no fun at all, with its uneven and slanted angles. Every turn is a new sensation of pain in my legs.

Trees tower over us and that familiar pine scent fills every breath. The road resembles two carved tracks with overgrown brush creeping its way over our shoulders. This simple path would be reclaimed in a couple weeks if Magnus didn't use it to travel from hub to hub. The roads are quiet now. We have yet to hear anything from the scouting vehicles up front. Caiden informed us earlier that they're watching out for patrols and transports, so we might not see them until just before we get to Talas. He tells me Magnus personnel rarely make trips unless they need to, only a patrol every week or so. Each hub is like a fortress so they aren't worried about much. Besides, whoever gets close enough might get caught in the hub's Influencer's web. This would just expand their collection of civilians. Our resistance is being shielded by the frontline Influencers, so we'll be ready for any push.

I've not seen Farren since we left the Walton hub. He's been up front brainstorming with Caiden and Miya. Should I be missing him like this? I feel like a little girl with a crush, but I can't help it. Amanda has been going on and on about all the people she has come across since joining the resistance. Whenever I get a moment of quiet, all I can think of is being alone with him again. It seems silly living in the world we live in, but what we're trying to do now can change everything. I need to focus and set aside these thoughts for now. Finding a comfortable spot to step has become my new obsession. I'm not built for these rugged hikes in the mountains.

A steady breeze caresses the path as it flows up the slope of the mountain. We've been going uphill for hours now and the higher altitude is not making things easy. The once thick wall of evergreen trees that surrounded us has thinned, revealing a peak at the crest of the mountain. Near the top, Amanda and I catch up to Farren and the other leaders. They sit on boulders and toppled trees. Looking around, I see the resistance resting all over the mountain top. They have broken off into groups and are now snacking on rations and passing around canteens while catching their breath. Turning back, I catch Farren grinning at me for a brief moment before he returns his eyes to Caiden. Before I have a chance to ask what is going on, Ava grabs my hand and pulls me away from the others. I look back and see Amanda give me a puzzled look. She's not used to others being involved in our lives. I don't even have a moment to think about this as Ava looks back at me and says, "Stop thinking and trust me."

Her long, athletic legs make navigating through the evergreen thickets and large boulders a breeze.

Hopping from rock to rock, never losing stride. If she wasn't assisting me I'm sure I would have broken something by now. We ascend for several minutes before we reach an opening that overlooks the Sierra mountain range. I swallow a gust of cool air and it fills my oxygen-deprived lungs. There is a purity to it that catches me off guard. Looking out at the endless horizon with its textured angles, the view puts this moment into perspective. The rocky peaks vault up through the lush, forested foothills and allow for an expansive view. It's been far too long since I have had a moment to really enjoy the simple elegance of life. Ava leans down and whispers in my ear, "Do you feel it?"

No, I don't, and that is what is so amazing. It's quiet and still. The complications of others aren't nagging at my inner peace. I turn to Ava and can only smile.

"It's something about the higher elevation," she says. "Owen says it's something to do with the electromagnetic field, but I don't care how, I just like it. Ever since I've been with Maddux, we spend most of our free time as high as we can get."

Amanda and I have always avoided these mountains. Magnus has infected this area like a virus. Predatory and invasive, they cling to whoever slips into their surroundings. Ripping freedom from their awareness and replacing it with mindless conformity. Even with the apparent danger, I can't imagine avoiding this anymore. It makes me feel normal in this less-than-normal world. Hopefully, after today, their ominous network will no longer entangle this beauty.

"Do you think we can really do this?" I ask. "I mean, we're just a small group of misfits up against an evil army."

Turning to me with that familiar look of calmness, she winks and says, "There's no such thing as misfits and evil armies. You keep forgetting reality is just a collection of thoughts and actions. Nobody is better at molding that than you. I'm not worried about it."

She might not be worried about it, but I sure am. No matter how much I have accepted my ability as a gift rather than a burden, I still don't believe I'm this almighty, powerful one they say I am.

"Let's get back to the group before Caiden eats all the rations." Ava's eyes brighten as she smiles.

We retrace our steps down the hillside and make it back to find that the group has already begun to move out. Farren calls out to me and greets us at the trail opening. "There you guys are," he says in between catching his breath. "I sent Caiden up the trail to check on the scout vehicles. Their last check-in signal is about fifteen minutes past due. I'm… I'm really starting to second guess having the group push forward."

"Do you think something's wrong?" I ask, scanning his face for a hint of fear.

"I don't know, maybe."

Just as I reach out to comfort him, fear overtakes his look of concern. The source of his worry reveals itself at the edge of the dirt path ahead.

"Stop... Stop... STOP," Caiden's voice intensifies with every bark. "The scout vehicles have been hit!"

18

HIDDEN CLARITY

CAIDEN'S FRANTIC YELL buckles the formations of the group as confused pockets of frontline resistance slam into another. Maddux, Caiden, and Owen rush back from the front, commanding the group to find cover. People hurry to the trees and road embankment. Splintered, the resistance breaks into small fragments of fighters, each looking for guidance and safety. Before the panic spreads to us in the rear, Farren stands in front of me forming a human shield. One arm holds a very large rifle while the other reaches around my waist, pulling me into his back.

"Stay with Ava," he commands as he releases his tight grip on my side. Within seconds he is sprinting ahead, darting through frantic resistance fighters. Ava pulls me to the nearest ditch and we take cover.

"Amanda... Where is Amanda?" I mutter under my breath.

I hear a loud crack that echoes through the forest. Creeping over the edge, I see one of the frontline fighters buckle to her knees. Then a second crack, and a third, fourth, fifth, the noise flooding through the foreground. Screams start to blend in with the gunshots and all I can hear now is chaos. People run in all directions looking for a more secure place to hide. The ringing in my ears is no match for the loud pops as more and more shots penetrate our location. Bodies fall to the ground. I can't see where the firing is coming from. All I can see is our resistance being picked off like a scattering herd of deer. Those who can't make it to the tree line are first to fall, then the people who are paralyzed in fear, unable to move from the ditch on the side of the road. Their shaking and frantic breathing stop as the bullets pierce their heads and limbs. Their fight is now over.

Ava tries to pull me off the embankment and into the woods, but I will not let her. Without thinking, I pry her fingers from my arm and run to find Amanda and Farren. Out of the corner of my eye, I catch a glimpse of a hazy object right before I am hit and knocked to the ground. Breathless and aching, I look up to see Farren's intense eyes locked on my face as his body lies on top of mine. The air rushes back into my lungs as he pulls me to my feet and off into the nearby thickets. "Keep your head down and stay put. Do you understand me?"

Farren gathers his weapon and once again makes his way toward the front. Taking cover from tree to tree, he narrowly reaches his destination. With all the madness I lose track of him. My heart sinks in my chest and tightness forms around my throat.

I can't think of my own safety right now. Farren is probably jumping in front of bullets to save people, and I'm sure Amanda is out there freaking out like I am. My eyes race back and forth and my breathing quickens as I think of what to do next. No more sitting around huddled in a ball—I need to help, somehow. Before I get a chance to test my bravery, Miya darts to Ava's and my side. She holds one of those large rifles that I have seen the frontline fighters carry. How her petite frame has the strength to carry it is beyond me. After reloading, she looks up at me and says, "Alright, young lady, I'm here to make sure you stay safe. Farren's orders."

When it comes to my family, I don't follow anyone's orders.

"There is nothing you can do right now," she shouts. "Whoever is shooting at us is protected by implants. Maddux has already tried flushing them out. And with all this firing, there isn't going to be an animal within miles to come to your rescue."

She is right; my *almighty* push ability is useless in a gunfight against sector group personnel. This isn't a bunch of mindless Harvesters with pitchforks and foul mouths. This is an army of organized, shielded, well-trained killers.

The blasts from the distance grow as more and more resistance start to fall. This ambush is plowing through our numbers. A pop bursts above our heads as shattered pieces of tree bark trickle down on us. This prompts Miya and Ava to guide us back deeper into the woods. With our heads hanging low we dart into the nearest clump of tall trees. Waiting around the thickest evergreen are the young Influencers Ava and I met with at the Walton hub. One of the older resistance members has taken responsibility for them in the disarray. Ava motions to them. "Guys, move now."

They rush to her like a flock of baby birds to their mother. Trevor and Envee are the first to put their arms around her. "What's going on?" Envee says to Ava while covering her ears.

The terror in their faces is tough to witness. Their eyes are so wide and their complexions are pale. "Breathe, guys, just breathe," Ava says while pulling them in closer.

All this does is remind me that Amanda is out there somewhere, scared, helpless, and most likely alone. That is when I get an idea. Trevor can find her with the help of Envee. His push can hone in on her to relay our messages while Envee can increase his reach with her ability.

I look up to Ava and say, "I need their help to find Amanda. I can't reach her in all this confusion."

"What are you thinking?" she asks.

After I explain my idea, she agrees and pulls back to get their full attention. "Alright, sweeties, it's your time to help the resistance. Kaylin needs you."

We all crouch down under the shelter of a fallen fir tree. Trevor looks to me and in a shaky voice asks, "What do you need me to do?"

He's so young, but among all the chaos he's still able to focus on me with his pure blue eyes.

"I need you to find my friend and send her a message. Can you do this for me?"

He looks to Ava for reassurance before turning to me. "I... I can do it."

I can barely hear his soft voice over the ongoing bursts of gunfire coming from every direction.

"Thank you," I smile. "Tell her to fall back, but have her go through the tree line just off the road. Make sure she understands we are back here waiting."

"Use Envee's ability to enhance your reach," says Ava.

"I'm ready, I'm ready, I'm ready," says Envee. Untamed energy spills from her.

Trevor nods to Envee and he shuts his eyes. Her hand softly rests on his shoulder in what she says is a way to link up with his push. He is trembling now more than before. "It's okay, we are protecting you," I say while resting a supportive hand on his other shoulder.

Being so young makes it easier for these kids to use their ability as there aren't as many complications bouncing around their minds. Of course, this situation is far from the ordinary. Gunshots and the cries of wounded people screaming for help must be hard to block out even for them. Less overthinking is one thing, but being so young amplifies your fears. That fear can consume your mind.

To my surprise, after a few seconds Trevor looks up and tells me it's done. I am shocked at how easy these kids can use their push ability even in the middle of this hectic battle. It's amazing how just a few years of maturity can screw with your clarity. I couldn't even focus long enough to get inside my own head during all of this, let alone extend out my push.

"That's it?" I ask, surprised.

"Yeah, she got the message," he insists.

Ava asks Terry, the man watching the kids, to take them deeper into the woods and wait for us. His round face and washed-out beard remind me of old magazine pictures I've seen of Santa Claus. He seems safe to me, and that is all I can hope for at this moment.

Ava and I make our way to a break in the trees that gives us a better vantage point. We can see the opening at the end of the path. Miya jumps from tree to tree and finds a ditch near the road. From there she will assess the battle and plan our next move. All we can hear are more gunshots all around us. We look ahead, waiting for Amanda, but only see our resistance fighters firing aimlessly into the trees ahead of our frontline. In between the patches of groundcover bursting into the air and branches snapping all around, I catch a glimpse of her.

It's Amanda. With her head covered by her arms, she runs with a purpose. Darting to the outer tree line, I lose sight of her. *She's alive, she IS alive.* I become antsy and try to shift to follow Amanda's movements. Ava grips my shoulders and shouts, "She will make it. You can't go after her now!"

My breathing hastens. All I can do is nibble on my lower lip and keep my head down. Ava's eyes are locked on mine. Her stare is holding me in place. That, plus she is physically much stronger than I am. It feels like it has been forever and the wait is killing me. My lock on Ava snaps as I hear Amanda rushing through the trees.

"Holy crap!" she says. "Whenever I leave you, the world explodes all over the place."

I yank her down onto me. My arms crush her as I squeeze all my fear out of my muscles. Releasing the pent-up emotions, my eyes brim with tears.

Amanda pulls back to look at me and asks if I am okay. We embrace for a little bit longer, but the cracks and bangs of gunfire all around pull our attention back to the battle. Ava rests a hand on each of our shoulders and guides us over to Miya at the embankment. We crawl the final few yards to her position. Glancing over the edge, we see just how intense the battle has become. Most of our fighters with weapons are firing blindly with no results. I haven't been able to feel anyone's awareness beyond the resistance. The enemy must all have the block implants. Our numbers have fallen, dead bodies stretching back across the dirt tracks we've been traveling on. Amanda tells me she saw Farren and the other leaders held up near the frontline. At least he—or I should say, they—are still alive. I don't have time to think about the complications my feelings for Farren have created. We are all trapped in ditches or crouched behind trees. Every few minutes a new scream rattles my body as someone else falls. Even Ava, who is never fazed by her surroundings, is scouring the landscape, popping her head up and down hoping to catch a glimpse of Maddux.

Miya looks over her weapon-free shoulder, her eyes scanning back and forth, and calls for our attention. "We're going to have to fall back into the woods."

What does she mean by that? Is this revolt over? Amanda and I have been exposed. We can no longer hide.

"Ava, I need you to make your way to the front and pull back as many of our numbers as you can. We need to retreat. There is no way to salvage this."

Ava takes a quick glance at me before nodding to Miya. With little effort she sprints from tree to brush to boulder and in a few seconds she's gone.

Amanda clings to me as if she knows Miya is going to command me to leave her. I will not go anywhere without her. My breathing has quickened and my throat is dry. I crouch into a ball with Amanda. Maybe I can at least use my push to calm her nerves. Waiting for a death order from Miya, I'm rattled from my push attempt. I turn to see Amanda's eyes bright and almost hopeful. Her gaze intensifies as she points to some nearby armed resistance fighters. I creep up to get a better view and see four or five heavily armed gunmen all synchronized and focusing their aim. Their faces are calm and determined. No sign of fear or desperation. Miya points up the path a little further to reveal more of our armed fighters blasting away with a purpose. That is when I feel it: a powerful push has blanketed the implant-free resistance. A heavy wash of warmth flows right through me. Amanda wiggles free from my softened hold and trains her sight out onto the tree line at the end of the tracks. She too has that clarity in her eyes. She turns to us and says, "Those dirtbags can't hide anymore."

The trees in the distance all start to shatter as our heavy gunfire pulverizes their limbs. Magnus fighters tumble from the tall pine and hemlock trees. Their bodies crash from branch to branch, kicking up groundcover as they pound the forest floor. Our pinpoint targeting is tearing through the concealed snipers. Miya follows the lead of the implant-free resistance and matches their firing patterns. Whoever's push this is has taken us from dying in ditches to owning this battle.

Within a few minutes, it is over. The firing has leveled off and now only a few fighters near the front continue to target the tree line. Not long after that the pops of the guns slow before the last shot is fired. Following this, a huge outburst of celebration comes from our resistance. Amanda is the first of our trio to join in with victory calls. Miya and I turn to each other, looking for answers. Without a word, I shrug my shoulders and give her a slight smile. Returning the smile, she rises from our roadside ditch and heads out toward the other fighters. Amanda takes my hand and pulls me out and onto the tracks. "It's over," she says. "They're all dead."

"Kaylin!" someone calls from up the path.

I turn my head to find Farren rushing to me as fast as he can. As he reaches us, he clenches my shoulders and pulls me to the side. His eyes scan me from head to toe. "You're alright, you're really okay," he says as he swallows down fatigue between heavy breaths.

I look up at his eyes and then quickly grab his waist, pulling myself into him. I rest my head on his chest and let the anxiety of the day melt away. His hand moves from my back to the arc of my neck while the other rests gently on my hip. This embrace does not last long as Ava, Maddux, and Caiden rush to us. Caiden's excitement pours out with curses and high fives. Farren pulls away from me. Ava's long arms swallow my body before she breaks away to return to Maddux. I rest an arm over Amanda's shoulders to soak up the celebration. Others from the resistance join us on the tracks. Curiosity pulls me over to Ava and Maddux as I ask, "How did you use your ability to find all those snipers?"

"It wasn't me," Ava says while turning to Maddux.

"Sorry, ladies, I can't take credit for this either. I thought for sure it was you, Kaylin."

"No, I was useless during all that," I say.

"Well, none of our other Influencers have that kind of push ability," Maddux insists.

That's when I feel something—someone—else. I recognize the same depth of consciousness I felt the first time I met him. It's full and warm and somehow familiar. I turn to look up the tracks toward the tree line and see him. Jax emerges from the flittering pine needles that still fall from the battle. Stepping over dead Magnus bodies as he reaches the path, he is ALIVE. The rest of the group catch on to what I am seeing and turns their attention on our returning leader. He looks well. Almost too well.

Moving toward each other, we meet on the path. Farren is silent, apparently in disbelief of Jax's return. The rest of the resistance behind us is now silent too, as they seem eager to hear him speak. Jax stops a few feet from us, his calm eyes assessing the group.

"I'm sorry I couldn't join you all sooner," he says. "I wasn't able to return or access communications."

Understandably, the group remains shaken by the battle, but still keep it together enough to hear him out.

"There's something happening at Talas," he continues. "The Magnus brothers have been very active of late. I wasn't sure if they uncovered my connection to the resistance. They had me out of the loop with the senior personnel. Some of the leaders and I were on lockdown for ten hours while they performed some sort of assessment of the staff."

The gathering stirs as Jax debriefs us. "They were going to inform us of some sort of major change, but that's when they received intel of your movements toward Talas."

"Those bastards knew our every step," shouts Caiden.

"I wasn't able to gather the details of the ambush," Jax says. "Since I was not involved in the planning, I could only track their snipers while keeping my distance. Once they set up, I had to wait for the battle to start to know our resistance was in range for my push.

"While gathering intel before I left Talas, I overheard the leadership crafting a plan to ambush us. I had to stay in order to get all the details."

You can feel a sense of relief as the group begins to piece everything together.

"Once I learned of this sniper assault, I had to follow them," Jax continues. "I've spent the last few hours trailing them. I knew they would wipe you all out once I saw them take position at the bottom of the mountain. They would see you far before you would see them."

Farren pulls himself from the crowd and stands to the right of Jax. He holds his hand up to get everyone's attention and says, "I know the losses are hard to take. We need to take a moment to tend to the dead."

The crowd has a look of defeat as they scan the battlefield, gazes landing on the bodies that have fallen around us. Some cover their mouths in disbelief while others just sob. I've seen enough death in the last few days; I fear I'm becoming numb to it.

Resting a supportive hand on Farren's shoulder, Jax adds, "We knew this resistance was not going to be easy. This battle was just a moment in the collective consciousness of our reality. The world just around the corner—a better world, one where we are free to live our lives and think our own thoughts—is what we're fighting for." He points down the path. "Now is the time to either fuel our fire or watch it trickle away to nothing. I choose to burn Magnus to the ground and free our family and friends."

The group has a collective sense of acceptance as people nod their heads. Murmurs and grunts of dedication rumble through the gathering. I can feel us once again coming together. People have lost friends and some have lost family, but there is no time to focus on that. Jax informs us that Magnus will know about what happened here soon enough. He asks us to take a moment, but to be prepared to move on to Talas within the hour.

Farren and Jax start directing people to bury the dead. Caiden and Miya coordinate efforts to salvage weapons and supplies.

Amanda takes my hand and leads me away from the others. We don't say a word to each other as we make our way to assist with the losses. She is quiet, her wit and sarcasm are gone. Her silence tells me everything I need to know about her emotions. We spend the next hour doing whatever we can to care for the fallen and wounded.

Barely a minute passes after the last body is buried before Jax insists we move to take out Talas. Farren walks with us now. He fills me in on what Jax is thinking. Magnus is vulnerable now. Their forces have been thinned because of this ambush. We either take on Talas now or let them call reinforcements from the nearby hubs. There is no time to think or discuss this. We're moving on and it will only get harder. The well-fortified Talas hub awaits us.

19

RESTART

TWENTY-ONE FIGHTERS and two Influencers were lost in the ambush. That's nearly a third of our numbers. None of us in the leadership were hurt. A trace of guilt washes over me. We didn't protect our people. I still don't feel like I'm really a part of the leadership. Maybe that's why the loss of life has become a constant pain in my gut. Thoughts of people shot in the head are unsettling. This pattern has not stopped since we started moving again. I have to find a better way to use my push when things get crazy. If not, more people will die. People are relying on me.

In the last functional scout vehicle, Caiden works with Owen on the new weapon tech we salvaged from the battle. The scout driver rolls next to the rest of us, who are on foot, matching our pace. Owen raves about how the guns are made of the wonder material, Graphene. As smart as he is, this guy is just as young as the rest of us and it shows. He grins as if he didn't just watch our people gunned down before his eyes. Either he doesn't really care about human life or he's too immature to feel the scope of what just happened.

One by one, Caiden calls up his best shooters to have them swap out their guns for the new ones. As if they're made of cardboard, he effortlessly tosses them to each fighter. How can something so powerful and precise be so lightweight? There's enough ammo left to arm ten fighters. The rest of the fancy guns are dismantled and tossed to the side of the tracks. More than twice of what's handed out is now roadside trash. Seems wasteful, but they're useless if you run out of bullets.

Incredibly light body armor is now distributed among the frontline fighters. There had to be forty or more snipers in those trees. Some are still dangling from branches as blood pours from their wounds to the forest floor below. For the most part, our remaining resistance received a much-needed upgrade. Maddux makes his way over to Farren, Amanda, and me with three armor vests in hand. Farren grabs one and fiddles with some display on the inner shoulder pad. He looks it over and holds it up to Amanda. She reaches out her arms to allow him to slip it on her narrow frame. The dark-gray vest covers her shoulders, chest, and core. The material itself adjusts to adhere to her body shape. She winces as it tightens.

Before he has a chance to adjust one for me I say, "I'll be fine; there aren't enough for everyone."

"Sorry, Kay, it's not your call," he insists as we follow behind the others.

"Aren't I one of the leaders? I want someone else to wear it."

The idea of leaving others unprotected while I get one doesn't sit well with me. They might call me part of this leadership, but I am still one of the newest members. Not that Farren would care if I told him that.

"Oh, thanks," Amanda says. "Way to make me feel like a selfish coward, Kaylin."

In a raised voice, Farren says, "Kaylin, please don't be stupid."

Kaylin? Stupid? Did he just go all full-first-name on me and then call me stupid? Before I have a chance to respond to that little nugget, Caiden comes up to Farren and grabs the vest from his hands. Without saying a word he forces my arms through the openings before adjusting it to my fit.

"Hey," I snarl. "What are you doing?"

As he walks away, he turns to me and says, "You and Farren saved my life at Hawthorne, so I owe it to him to keep you alive."

Huffing for a moment, I eventually give in and accept the vest.

Farren checks the fit before he notices my gaze. Looking up at him with a halfhearted glare, I say, "I'm stupid, huh?"

He avoids my eyes, and it's probably for the best.

Amanda makes her way to the support members, as Caiden calls them, near the back. Maddux and Ava join us as we make our way up to the front, where Jax and Miya lead the march. The resistance, while thinned out, still can have an overwhelming presence. We fill the dirt pathway that leads to Talas. The tracks slope slightly down, packing us in tighter as we slow to control our descent. Jax hasn't sent the scout vehicle ahead because he knows Magnus is expecting us now. It has been about two hours since the ambush began. The snipers would've reported back by now if they weren't all half-naked and dead on the side of the road. They didn't get the proper burial our own fallen received. Knowing Jax and Farren, they probably would have if it wasn't for a lack of time. We are not the Magnus Order.

We march on as heavily armed fighters surround us. The leadership strategizes up front. With the element of surprise now gone, we need to reassess.

Caiden has made his way from the scout vehicle to join the discussion. Farren tells us we have about an hour before we get to Talas. This doesn't leave us much time. Farren suggests we break the resistance into smaller groups and take the hub from all access points. Caiden likes this, as it gives him more ways to use tactics. His face lights up at the thought. Miya isn't so sure. She believes this will just weaken us, taking away the newly sniper-free advantage. She suggests we take them head on. Jax agrees with her. Both of them have the most knowledge of the inner workings of the Talas hub. If anyone's going to know how this hub will react, it's Miya and Jax. How they could have worked so closely with Magnus without dying a little bit inside is crazy to me. Maybe they did. I still don't know them all that well.

It's midday, the sun filtering through the overhanging evergreens. The scout vehicle hums as it crawls in front of the group now. Two gunmen stand ready out of the open sunroof. This provides us with a bit of a shield if Magnus has any new surprises waiting.

Jax asks if I can use my ability to scan the area for the awareness of anyone unfamiliar. Beyond our group, it's peaceful. I only pick up the faint haze of wildlife as it scurries throughout the woods. Ghostly images scatter just out of my direct eyesight as these creatures sneak into my awareness. It's like seeing a shadow of the animal as it filters through the forest around me. In this case, these faint shadows phase through the trees and natural landscape. I can never directly see them. The moment I turn to look at them, normal conscious reality once again fills my awareness. It's like looking straight ahead, but always seeing something hazy just out of your direct sightline. Luckily, I have to open myself up to it in order to feel the nearby awareness of others. If not, I would always be feeling paranoid. Shadowy figures lurking around me at all times would be creepy. It's all clear for now, but I will keep my antenna up just in case.

Amanda has become comfortable with her assignment. It appears she enjoys people a lot more than she did just a few days ago. Her trust in this resistance has come a long way. Before, she was always hanging by my side looking out for me. I don't get that maternal attitude as much anymore. It's nice, but I miss her, too. I turn to find her chatting with a couple of frontline guys. Her smile warms my heart. These two young guys laugh as they peer over her. Their interest looks genuine. Amanda flirting with guys—that's just odd to me. I hope I'll see this side of her again after this next battle.

"Okay, hold up here for a bit." Jax turns, holding his hand up to the group. "I'm starting to feel the consciousness of the Talas civilians."

I don't feel them. His reach is truly amazing. No wonder Magnus expanded so fast with him at the helm. He was a super-charged beacon, pushing the evil agenda of the Magnus Order. That just sounds scary, even though I believe I know the real Jax now. His heart seems to be pure. Forced to do something against your will is all part of being an Influencer in today's world.

"We're about five miles out. We need to be prepared," he says.

Caiden and Maddux call the frontline fighters and Influencers over to a small clearing just off the tracks. He has everyone check their weapons and look over supplies. When he's not goofing around, Caiden can really be intimidating with the way he gets in the faces of those not prepared. Out of the corner of my eye, I see Miya and Jax turn their attention to me and Ava. Nerves tighten my throat as the reality of what is going to happen soon sinks in. A cough clears my airway as I prepare for what is next.

"Hi, Kaylin," Jax says with a simple smile. "Sorry I haven't had a chance to talk with you since my return."

"Hey," is all that slips out of my mouth. *Seriously, Kaylin, is that all you can think of to say?*

"Hi, guys, what's the plan?" Ava says.

"Nice to see you again, Ava," Jax replies. "Well, we need you to gather all the backline Influencers. We need them ready to react to our first attack."

He shifts his focus between us. The relaxed manner in which he leads emits confidence.

"You two need to direct the young ones however you see fit. Miya and I will be trying to locate the Magnus leadership. I won't be able to guide your efforts. You two must protect this group. Do not put yourself or these kids in the line of fire. Your abilities will be vital to winning this battle."

Ava and I have already discussed how to use each of our abilities to help, so when that time comes we will be ready. What I'm concerned with is Amanda's safety.

"What about Amanda and the rest of the civilians who aren't on the front line?" I ask.

Miya adjust the weapon slung over her tiny shoulder and volunteers to answer my question. "Well, honey, our fighters will need support. Most of those who aren't fighting have been trained to help the wounded or to supply ammo and resources. Just make sure she knows where to be when the fighting starts. Can you do that, dear?"

I still am not a fan of how she talks to me. It's almost like she thinks of me as a burden or a delicate flower.

"Um, yeah I'll talk to her."

Ava tells me she is going to gather the backline Influencers to get them ready. I tell her I will be there in a minute. I need to find Amanda and make sure she's ready.

To my surprise, I find her already working with people at the weapons stash. She's got a clipboard and it looks like she is managing inventory. She glances over her shoulder and gives me a corny smile and says, "Hey, Kay, look at me. I'm useful."

The resistance is humming now. Everyone is where they need to be. Making my way to the back, I see Ava, Envee, Trevor, and the four other Influencer kids gathered together. Several armed fighters surround them. That makes me feel a little less scared. Not much, but at least a little. I join them and we go over what we discussed at the Walton hub. Everyone knows their role. Making it happen is what I'm worried about.

Only a few minutes pass before I hear my name called. It's Farren. He rushes from the middle of the group. Two rifles crossed over his broad shoulders. Sweat dampens the front of his sleeveless T-shirt, revealing the hardened contours of his chest. I divert my attention only to return my gaze immediately. I'm glad he ditched those stiff Magnus clothes at the Walton hub. He pulls me a few steps from the others, off to the side of the tracks, just behind a grove of trees. I look up at him and before I have a chance to say anything, his warm hand caresses the back of my neck. He pulls me closer into his body. Looking up at his intense brown eyes, we lock on the same thought. He inches dangerously close and then it happens. His lips feel chapped, but still amazingly soft as they connect with mine. His hand intertwines in the hair just above my ponytail. Cautious at first, I slowly put my arms around his waist. It only lasts a few seconds before he pulls back a bit. Flush with warmth that flows over my body; I pull my right hand from his back and place it in the center of his chest where his heart beats rapidly against the palm of my hand. Looking up at him, I have nothing to say. Words have lost their meaning. Looking down at me, his messy hair dangles in front of his brow. He exhales as if he has been holding his breath forever. He releases me and darts back into the crowd, calling back over his shoulder.

"Be safe for me."

20
NEW MOTIVATION

"SOMETHING TO FIGHT for, huh?" Ava says just before pursing her lips.

The girls in our group snigger. I guess Farren and I didn't go deep enough into the woods. I take a deep breath and return to the kids.

Just as fast as the kiss happened, the mood is reversed. Caiden informs each pocket of the resistance that we're moving out. I look up ahead to see the group move in sections. The frontline fighters lead the way with their Influencer support just a few steps behind. Led by Caiden, our newly armored snipers break off into three packs. We still have a few miles to travel, but we're not going to be caught off guard again.

A large group of armed men and women flank Jax and Miya just behind the first wave. Their objective is simple: locate the Magnus Order leadership. Besides them, Farren is the only person in this group who has any information about the corporate head of this sector group. I just assume the heads of Magnus are sitting at the top of a gold tower plotting evil or something.

Amanda, Owen, and the rest of the support members hang back quite a bit from Jax and Miya's position. The scout vehicle hauls supplies in front of them while providing a bit of cover for the small group. Amanda has a couple of well-placed armed fighters right next to her. If there's any spot in this resistance that is actually safe, it would be there. She is talking to Owen about some of the tech he's invented. I didn't realize they knew each other.

That just leaves our Influencer team and armed escorts to bring up the rear. With things in place and the rumble of footsteps pressing forward, it's getting harder to not freak out.

I can't help but think about Farren now. He jumps from the frontline to Jax's group as he makes sure everyone is okay. I see him talking to Maddux and that takes me out of my self-centered bubble. Ava hasn't said a single word about him or shown any concern for what is coming. She holds Envee's hand as we walk. She is nearly twice her size, but even with her daunting presence she's still able to show a great deal of care for those around her. I walk faster to catch up and ask, "How's Maddux doing?"

She takes my hand and we all walk together.

"Maddux and I have been together for a long time now," she says. "We've been through a ton of battles. We've learned that if we're going to survive, we need to be at our best and do what we do."

Her frayed, wavy dark hair almost sparkles in the light that peers through the trees. "That means we need to focus on our abilities, not each other. It might sound harsh, but I want to hold him in my arms again and to do that I need to be at my best."

This hits me hard. Caught up with my feelings for Farren, I realize that I've done very little preparation for using my push. Influencers need a clear mind to affect the collective consciousness of others. It's time to grow up and understand where I am and what I'm about to do. That's all it takes to get my head straight. I'm motivated now.

21

MAGNUS INSIGHT

IT'S BEEN QUIET for the last hour. The path has leveled off and we've been taking it slow as we keep our eyes and ears on our surroundings. We're less than a mile out now. The civilians at the hub are flickering in my consciousness, but I don't sense any hectic activity on the horizon. That lack of movement is starting to worry me. Jax must be feeling the same thing. He makes his way to my group. Under his command, everyone stops for a much-needed rest.

"Kaylin, do you have a minute?" he asks.

Knowing what he's thinking, I turn to him and say, "Yeah, you feel it too, don't you?"

"I do, I do," he says. "I've been feeling the civilians for the last couple of hours and something's just not right. There doesn't seem to be a sense of urgency with them. Have you picked up anything else?"

Even though his reach is far greater than mine, neither of us are close enough to piggyback on the visual thoughts of the people in the hub. All we can really sense is movement and the size of the group.

"No, I haven't," I reply. "We need to get closer."

"I might need to get closer, but you don't."

It takes a second before I understand what he's saying. Then it clicks. I don't know why I didn't think of it earlier: I need to connect with my little forest friends.

"Birds!" I say while I grab his shoulders. "Birds."

A smile is all it takes for him to show me that we're now on the same page. I remove my hand and wonder if my over-eager reaction may have been too much. He's a calm guy who doesn't appear to be easily rattled. It's just comfortable around him.

"Have Envee help you cover as much of the area in and around Talas as you can," he advises.

After waking up my brain, he heads over to the Influencer kids. Even with so much responsibility, he still spends a few moments encouraging them while he waits for my nature outreach.

Jax exchanges a fist bump with Trevor and says, "You're doing a great job here."

Even though Trevor only comes up to Jax's elbow, there's a maturity in the way he handles the world. They are a lot alike.

"I'll check back with you and the others later," says Jax.

Envee and I step outside the pack as the resistance settles in for a break. Less distraction is always best when using your push. I've informed her of what I want to do and she's excited, even jumpy. This kid has no shut-off switch. Once I tell her it's time to get started, it's like she channels all that energy into the push. We hold hands as we find a tree to sit against. She tells me she's ready. Her fragile fingers get lost in my grasp. A sweet smile peers up at me. And just like that, she's calm.

Being amplified is an odd sensation. Beyond my normal sense of expanding consciousness, I feel pulses of deeper reach. As each wave expands beyond me, more life enters my push. Short, rapid breaths increase the pounding coming from my chest. Envee's focused, high energy is somehow penetrating my body. All sorts of life flashes before my mind as hazy objects burst in from all angles. I've never experienced so much connection before. The wildlife that inhabits this area dwarfs the clustered consciousness from the resistance. Envee's ability blends with my push so well that she disappears from my reality completely. The only way I know she's here is by the way my push has been enhanced.

Within a few moments, I see a vision of endless blue sky. The horizon stretches out beyond the mountains before fading into the atmosphere. Extending out from this body are wings that gather the air pushing me higher. Complications fall away as I connect with the purity of an eagle. Its movements are different from other animals, more free. It's like they have more options to explore the world. Flying frees you from the limitations of land travel. I feel less barriers and more openness. The first time I connected to birds, I didn't understand what was happening. Now I have a chance to enjoy glimpses of their reality. Slipping from the eagle's consciousness, I hone in on a flock that's much further up the path. Their conscious ripples are tiny compared to the abundant life that hides in the woods near our group. The flock is easy to push as their minds are simple and don't affect reality like people do. They just live in the moment and the environment they're given. The simplicity of their existence makes this easy for me.

Flashes of visual thoughts flicker in from the birds' connection—expansive vistas stretching as far as the horizon allows. With a simple shift in my mindset, I've steered them toward Talas. Without the limitations of ground travel, they cover vast distances in no time to follow my push. I'm starting to recognize the surroundings of this area. The tattered tracks just before the hub come into focus. No one is patrolling the area, not even a scout vehicle. We must have weakened them more than we thought. Can this really be this easy? An image of the towering walls of the hub bursts before my mind's eye. The thick cement wall encircles the intimidating structure. More and more thoughts flutter in. The structure is huge, much bigger than the Hawthorne or Walton hubs. Reaching at least ten stories high, the main building resembles a cement fortress. The Magnus leadership must have a Napoleon complex—this place is unnecessarily large. Besides a few guards patrolling the outer wall and inner opening before the hub, there's not much movement. One by one, the birds' ripples fade as I pull away from the push.

Envee's hand is clammy now. I must've been holding on a bit too tight. Her eyes are closed. She's unaware I've stopped the push. Once I release my hand, her eyes flutter before they lock onto mine. My subtle nod and smile are all that is needed for her to understand that the push worked. Unfocused energy surges back to her body as she returns to the others. Her pace quickens with every step as she dashes to Ava. Jax notices Envee's return and heads my way.

"How are the birds feeling today?" he jokes.

"Simple, worry-free, and nothing like me."

His hands rest on his side now, in what I like to call a power pose. Again, it's nothing like my presence. He laughs confidently. Strands of my loose, oily hair tickle my nose. This annoyance prevents me from looking as cool as him. I bat the hair from my eyes in what must look like a convulsion. I gather myself and say, "There's not much going on up there around Talas. Not much at all."

His glance diverts from mine as he takes in what I say. After a moment to digest my words, he says, "Well, that's not good. Something's up, and knowing Magnus like I do, it's not going to be a pleasant return."

"What do you think they're planning?" I ask.

"Well, they tend to have a treasure trove of evil countermeasures on hand."

Even the former head Influencer of the Magnus Order doesn't know everything about our enemy. That's not a fun thought. I once again invite my favorite friend—worry—to consume my thoughts.

"Only Harold and Percy really know what is going to happen when we get there," he says.

"Who the heck are Harold and Percy?" I ask.

Realizing my limited knowledge of this sector group, he stops to fill me in. He tells me that they are the Magnus brothers. They founded this sector group. They were very rich and prominent figures just before the collapse of society a few decades back. They not only built the massive Talas hub, named after their favorite childhood pet, but they built a bunch of other hubs in the area for their powerful buddies. They created a safety network for the elite, which they later exploited in order to control this new world. Those who didn't follow their lead were overrun and forced outside to deal with the reality the Magnus brothers had helped create.

Jax goes on to tell me that Percy is the older brother; his intelligence can't be overlooked. But Harold is the vicious leader who ran the newly founded Magnus Order like a greedy corporation of the past. He was determined to gain as much ground as possible and they both knew Influencers were the key. It's believed that the Magnus Order was the first sector group to start collecting young talent for the sole purpose of expansion and control. This started the Influencer recruiting war that basically forced groups to gather young kids with push abilities. Not adopting these tactics would certainly lead to the devouring of your sector group. Magnus operates like an empire with consciousness-shaped servants believing they're living a safe and free life. But the truth is far more desperate. Everything Jax tells me is only reinforcing my decision to join this fight. The next step is to prepare ourselves for the unknown.

22

THE GATES OF TALAS

OUR FINAL PUSH to Talas has begun, but not everyone will be joining us. The leadership has set up a small camp for the wounded and the older members of our resistance. As planned from the beginning, a few guards stay behind to watch a small group that has set up just off the tracks near a sheltered dropoff. Rocks and trees protect them from all angles. An older lady named Lorraine attends to the injured under a makeshift shelter made of tarps and blankets. She traveled with us from Maddux's camp. She's quiet but has some medical training, which is all that matters now. I recognize a few other faces, but most everyone I'm close to will be risking their lives in this final battle. If we succeed, we will return for them. 'If' is a scary word, but I don't have the confidence to say 'when.' The next stop will be the Magnus Order's gates.

Breaking away from my group, I find my way to the scout vehicle. I need to see how Amanda is handling all of this. She's hard at work, lugging supplies into the truck.

"I'm sorry I haven't been able to check on you," I say.

She puts down a box of ammo in the bed of the truck and turns to me. "Kay, I should be checking on you. I don't care if you've just discovered you can shoot lasers out of your eyes or whatever, you are still my little sister."

It hasn't taken her long to find her niche as she loads sniper bullets into the spare magazines. I shouldn't be surprised; she's always been able to adapt to whatever situation we came across.

Taking her arm, I pull her away from her duties. Her eyes hold mine as I say, "Just know I love you and I'm grateful for all that you've done for me."

"Hey, I love you too, but just because you found a cute boy, don't think you can get rid of me." She smiles as she wraps her arms around me.

"Wait, what did you hear?"

She grins. "Get back to work, soldier!" she says, avoiding the question.

Everyone has returned to their assigned groups. As for that *cute boy*, we've both kept busy. That is by design, as we need to stay focused.

Ava and I have been preparing the young Influencers. We don't want them to be caught off guard and unable to use their push when needed. Honest, yet scary, insights are given to them by design. The more they know now, the less likely they are to lock up under pressure. This tactic helps me as well. We tell them how there might be more deadly gun battles and how more lives could be lost. Ava knows more than anyone how push ability can turn sane people crazy. One of our biggest responsibilities is to protect the implant-free members of the group, as well as the innocent Talas civilians. The kids seem to be ready, but children's emotions can be fragile. Ava and I will look out for them.

Caiden calls out to the group to begin the final march to Talas. With about a half mile to go, anything can happen now. Strategic gaps separate the different parts of the resistance. This should help keep us from being one big target. To me, we just look like three or four big targets instead. My throat is dry and my stomach is churning. Our armed escorts are eager to move while the rest of my group is slow to start. Not wanting to be the last one out, I take a deep breath, exhale, and lead my group forward. Ava pats me on the back to show she's proud of me. I take one last glance at the people left behind, ignoring the momentary envy I feel, and turn back to focus on the slow progress of the resistance. Each step is another second closer to blood, death, and more chaos.

***

"Frontline: take positions," Farren commands from the cover of a tree at the bend in the path.

Snipers and armed fighters flow out the front like water from a hose. They spread across the visible foreground, taking whatever vantage point they can find. Just around the corner is the outer gate to the Talas hub. It's getting intense now.

The plan is to take the gate by sheer numbers. This will give Jax, Miya, and their team an entry point through which they can go find the leadership. How they do that once they get in is beyond me. My team is tasked to disrupt and protect the group with our abilities. We weren't overwhelmed with tons of details on purpose. They need us to concentrate and not overthink.

Talas civilians are still going about their routine with little change from when I first picked them up an hour ago. Not knowing what's coming is freaking me out. A young girl rushes from the frontline back to us. I don't recognize her. She relays a quick message from Maddux.

"There are three active Influencers in or around the hub. Stay sharp."

His ability has helped us to better understand what we're dealing with. If we can counter their pushes during the battle, then there's a good chance our fighters can overtake the hub. Ava says their Influencer network has always lacked the unique skillset of our resistance. From what she's heard, they're nothing more than a bunch of mood shifters.

Ava pulls us over to a small grove of hemlock thickets just off the tracks. From here, we'll see the attack on the outer gate. Just like the Hawthorne hub, Talas has an outer wall that leads into a courtyard. This open area is like a moat without the water. Cleared of overgrowth, this surround is about forty yards deep and circles the entire main structure. It makes for a perfect spot for snipers to pick off our people from above.

Shielded from the gates, the support members take cover behind the scout vehicle. Amanda catches me looking over. In classic Amanda form, she gives me a silly grin followed by a thumbs up. She has always used wit to mask her fears. At least she is away from the action. Farren, on the other hand, waits for Caiden's signal to charge the gates of Talas. Clutching his rifle, he appears locked in and ready to strike.

A swift point from Caiden and the frontline move in. I'm too nervous to blink. Five armed fighters crouch as they spill out from the bend. Covering the few yards, they slam up against the cement outer wall to the right of the gate. There's still no sign of Magnus countermeasures. The men and women with the sniper rifles take the spots the charging fighters left behind. From one knee they look to provide cover fire when needed. Farren signals for the group's Influencers to move up. I need to stop watching him so much and keep my awareness open. Maddux leads this small group into a closer vantage point just off Farren's location. Just as they reach him, Farren raises his weapon to his shoulder and points it toward the gate. My breathing picks up as he explodes toward the wall to join the fighters. I need to help him now.

Once again, I open my awareness onto the hub, but there is still no one to connect to. All I sense is the generic movement of civilians, nothing else. They have to be shielded by a Magnus Influencer, as the conscious ripples that surround them are tightly contained to each individual. There is no open mind to piggyback from. Ava has been unable to alter the mindset of any unprotected Magnus supporters, as well. Something is up, but there doesn't seem to be a way to find out with our abilities. Envee has been amplifying the reach of Kelen and Deeya with no luck. They've been focusing on gathering any intel about the civilians that they can. Ava, the kids, and I are failing hard. We need to get our fighters inside to see what is really going on.

Loud pops make me flinch as hissing sounds fill the foreground. Caiden shouts out just outside the entrance, "Smoke grenades!"

Jax and his team scramble back to the edges before the bend. Dark smoke drifts from the wall and clouds our vision. I no longer see Farren or the other fighters near the gate. A cluttered echo of disjointed commands rumbles from the front.

The guards corral the support members to the rear of the scout vehicle. Amanda sits against the rear tire covering her ears. I want to rush to her, but she's in about as safe a spot as anyone. I need to find out what's going on up front. Without thinking, I lunge from the covering and sprint to the bend. Ava calls out for me to stop, but it's too late, I am gone. She has to protect the young Influencers and won't come after me. I sprint several yards and lean up against a granite boulder that shields me from the chaos just outside the gate. From here I can hear more clearly. I make out Farren shouting at the other fighters at the wall to stay put. Between wisps of smoke, I see Caiden holding his arm out to keep everyone else back. Farren and the others are alone now.

I wait for a rain of bullets that never comes. Several more smoke grenades clank as they hit the ground, followed by increased clouds of gray. What's the point of this? What are they up to?

Jax and Miya rattle me out of my lock on the haze. Gasping for air, Miya yanks my hand and says, "Why are you out of position?"

Jax interrupts her. "Kaylin, this isn't the plan. What are you doing?"

"Sorry, guys." I keep my eyes locked forward, still searching for Farren. "I won't hide back there if he's in danger."

Unlike her normal holier-than-thou attitude, Miya grabs my other hand and forces me to look at her. "Hon, he means a lot to me too. Maybe not in the same way, but what I'm saying is that I understand. We just have to be smart now."

They might be right, but it doesn't feel right to just stay behind this wall and do nothing. Before they have a chance to go on, a blast erupts from the gate. The burst dissipates the cloud of smoke from the area. We turn to see a mangled entrance jarred open and Farren and our fighters taking cover on either side. Farren must have been tired of waiting around choking on smoke. I want to call out to him, but that wouldn't be smart. It could distract him or, even worse, expose the resistance's position.

"Fall back, fall back!" A command echoes from someone in the clearing over the wall.

We've taken the front gate with little effort. Not even a bullet has been fired. This is starting off way too easy. That nervous feeling in my gut tells me there is more going on here.

With the gate breached, Caiden leads his fighters to Farren's position. He calls out for the snipers to eye the roof of the inner structure from inside the wall. Caiden and Farren's teams work together now. Several heavily armed resistance funnel through the gate.

Jax and Miya instruct me to stay put as they make their way to their support team at the outer wall just off the gate. Well, that's not going to happen. After a slight hesitation, I move from the protection of the bend. Hunched over, I follow behind their team. I blend in with the fighters and find a spot on the wall. Everyone is too concerned with the fight to notice an out-of-place, unarmed Influencer. This is probably the most stupid thing I've ever done.

"All clear," says one of the snipers as she finishes a scan of the rooftop.

Jax and his team begin to move through the gate. Nudged from all sides, I become one of the cattle herded through the entrance. This opening is a great choke point for Magnus to pick us off, but still nothing happens. I pass through the seared gate, its edges glowing hot from the blast. The exposed skin on my arm comes inches from the torched metal. There's no settlement wing to navigate. Talas doesn't do sorting, all their recruits come pre-vetted from Hawthorne or from the other entry hubs. We clear the gate and fan out into the opening. Farren has already moved fighters to the main structure. He's unaware of my foolish actions. I'm not that lucky with Jax, as he rushes over to me near the inner wall.

"Kaylin, what are you doing here?"

I feel like an orphan getting scolded by a shelter supervisor. I try to explain why I'm here, but all I can think of is Farren. Then it comes to me.

"You know something's not right," I plead. "Our Influencers are useless outside the gate."

I struggle to keep my eyes on him as my focus is pulled to Farren, who's on the other side of the clearing. He waves and points people into position near the hardened hub walls. I see him barking orders as his group falls into place.

"I need to know what's going on so I can use my push to help," I say.

Even if my intentions are not solely dedicated to the battle, I am right and he knows it.

Not having time to talk me out of it, he turns from me and says, "Please just stay close to me and my team."

And just like that, I am now one of the frontline fighters about to storm the deadly Magnus headquarters.

23

NOT SO FAST

OUTSIDE THE TALAS gates, Ava, the Influencers, Amanda, and the support members all remain. The rest of us are flush with the walls of the structure waiting for the next move.

Caiden and Farren's now-combined group is up ahead edging their way to the east entrance. Their movements remind me of our rescue mission for Amanda. They use the base of the hub to stay concealed while moving. Snipers pop on and off the wall as they keep an eye on the rooftops. Maddux and the frontline Influencers have joined their route. I don't see a hint of fear in him. His face isn't tense and his movements are slow and controlled. There's no wasted effort with him. Maddux and Ava are both older, which means they have been living as active Influencers for much longer than me. This explains why nothing seems to faze them. They've been tapped into the collective consciousness of others for so long that they must be able to anticipate behavior much more easily. This gives them the confidence to overcome crazy odds. However, I'm not so sure with everything so greatly stacked against us.

Jax and Miya are taking turns checking on me. Thirty seconds don't go by without one of them looking back at me to make sure I haven't somehow scaled the walls or something. My new wildcard attitude is making them nervous. The possibilities of what Farren and I could be is fueling this new sense of purpose. I know I can be much more effective closer to the action. Being useless beyond that wall is not an option. So, let's hope overthrowing Magnus is as easy as busting our way through that outer gate. I doubt it, though.

A heavy pressure engulfs my heart. The sensation rips the air from my lungs. A powerful push has just begun, and it's not like anything I've felt before. I bend over and grab my knees to support my weakened body. Sadness overtakes my thoughts. The awareness of the area is dulled and the mood is somber, yet desperate. This push doesn't affect me directly, but tapping into the collective fold of the area sends glimpses of despair to my mind. Pops of visual experiences flicker before me. Immersed within my mind, these bright explosions fill my inner thoughts. Glimpses of blurred memories come and go within a second of each other. They come and go so fast that it's hard to understand what's happening. This is making it impossible to counter this unfamiliar push.

A loud crack vibrates from the structure wall. I flinch and cover my ears before I turn to see one of our fighters crumble to the ground. There's a small pistol in his hand and a gushing hole above his brow. With blood splattered on the fighters nearest to him, the resistance jump from the mysterious event in shock. Covering my mouth, I try not to scream. I don't understand—this fighter just took his own life.

Without a second to process what happened, a woman runs into the clearing, forcing her own rifle into her mouth. Panicked shouts from the wall beg her to stop, but it is too late. The bullet rips through the back of her head. Momentum from the blast forces her body backward before she falls.

Confusion paralyzes the group. Panning from side to side, I watch people looking to their neighbors in panic. Most of them pull their weapons in close to their bodies. Murmurs of fear ramp up as two others cry out before ending their own lives. The formation of the group is tearing apart.

Jax rushes into the clearing, his arms outstretched, pleading with them to stay put. Noticing this, I see Farren pull out from the wall, aiming his weapon at the rooftop.

"Focus on me," Jax cries. "Someone is using their push ability on you."

He might not feel a push's reflection the same way I can, but I'm sure he understands the uniqueness of what is happening. He shuffles up and down the line, trying to catch the attention of as many as he can.

"What you're feeling is not real," he insists. "I need everyone without an implant to lower your weapons to the ground, now."

You don't need to be an Influencer to feel the unease from everyone. We all look to our fellow fighter to wait for someone to act first. Then Caiden pulls out from the gathering toward Jax and Farren. His pace is slow. One hand clasps the back of his neck while the other holds a pistol. Uncertain of his intentions, Farren calls out for him to be the example for those without the protective block implant. "Caiden," urges Farren. "Focus on me and drop your gun, okay?"

Our collective lock on Caiden breaks as Tarex, one of the weapons trainers I briefly worked with, drops to his knees, sobbing. A large rifle draped across the back of his neck supports his arms. His eyes are shut as tears stream down his face.

Before he has the chance to act on his misery, Caiden stops a few feet in front of him. With a blank look on his face, he raises the pistol to Tarex's head. Cries of confusion and fear drown out the calls from Jax in the clearing.

I'm able to make out what Caiden says. "It's okay, brother, it will be over soon."

With Caiden never being an official part of a sector group, his implant-free mind is vulnerable. The push has taken hold of him. I can't catch my breath. Everything is falling apart so fast.

Without thinking, I barrel through frightened fighters toward Caiden. I disconnect from the morbid awareness affecting the area. *This can't happen, please don't let this happen.* I only make it a few yards before Farren slams him to the ground. The weapon discharges into the air as it flies several yard into the clearing. I flinch and almost trip, but manage to steady myself.

"What the hell are you doing?" Caiden asks, shaking his head.

The hit has broken him from the effects of the push. He's clearly not sure what's going on.

"Are you with me, brother?" Farren asks, still on top of him.

"Get off of me," Caiden barks.

Farren slides off and helps him to his feet. You can see in Caiden's eyes that he realizes he was being influenced. He seems embarrassed. Farren peers over Caiden's shoulder to find me just outside the line. He moves Caiden aside and, glaring at Jax, stomps over to me. I guess he doesn't believe I'm capable of disobeying orders on my own. With a scowl on his face, he grabs my arms and quickly looks me over for injuries. Before he has a chance to say anything, another resistance member retrieves Caiden's pistol. The woman is picking up where Caiden left off. She heads toward Tarex mumbling something about how it's the right thing to do. Her eyes have that same dead look to them. Diverted, Farren bear hugs the woman and wrestles the weapon free. This isn't going to be the end of this. The push will only continue to invade the reality of the unshielded at this wall. Enough's enough.

Rage brims inside me. My push has awakened. The emotion pent up in my belly fuels the expansion of my consciousness. Intense flickers of light streak across the darkness behind my closed eyes. Awareness floods over the Talas hub. It bypasses the simple mental ripples and I dive deeper into the manipulated reality of the area. The people sharing this forced reality burst before me. Large expanded ripples of individuals affected by this push fuse my focus onto them. Whoever is creating this altered reality is grabbing hold of unshielded resistance and shifting their mood to a horrid place. The dark push transfers from one mind to another so quickly that I'm unable to latch on to anyone long enough to counter it. All I see are quick explosions of darkened ripples bursting before my mind. They retract just before the next innocent mind suffers the same entanglement. The frustration fuels my ability, making it possible to match the dark push. I'm able to anticipate the next victim just as it starts. *I've got you now.* Each fighter in our group is diffused and brought back to their own individual piece of reality. The collective focus of the group is calm once again. I stay engaged until the evil push fades from the area.

My eyes flutter open as if I'm waking from a long nap. Farren is hunched over me, and his head shifts a bit as he tries to catch my attention. I'm able to disconnect from the effects of the push just as I find his dark gaze. An easy smile breaches the concern on his face.

"So…" He pauses. "I'm assuming you must have changed their reality?"

Exhaling in relief, I simply nod yes to him.

We both take a second to look over the group. They're reforming the line against the wall. Once again, they focus on the mission. Only the Influencers and shielded are standing around trying to piece things together.

"Sorry I couldn't warn you," I say. "You could only take down so many at a time."

I clasp onto a few of his fingers and pull closer to him.

"I know you like tackling people and all, but we have a mission to take care of here." I chuckle.

He smiles, rolling his eyes. It feels good to be with him again. I don't like being in the back of the group. All I do there is fear for his safety.

Besides Farren, Maddux and the other Influencers are the first to catch on to the altered reality. There's no explanation needed for them. They get back to protecting the group with an even more heightened awareness. My defensive push has forced them to be alert at all times. We need to work together to overcome whatever sinister plans Magnus has in store for us.

24

DECISIONS

"**WE NEED TO** reevaluate here, guys," insists Jax.

The leadership, including myself, need to decide if we should send the implant-free fighters back to the safety outside the gates. Positioned near the support vehicle, Owen has confirmed there's been no one in their group affected by the morbid push. It appears the deadly power of this push is limited to a small radius near us. That's good news, I guess.

Caiden, the only one of the leadership not implanted, is pushing hard to keep our numbers strong with the full group. "That freak did that suicide crap to me and the rest of us for a reason," he says. "They want us thinned out to make us weak."

"He's right," says Maddux. "This kind of evil needs to be stopped."

If anyone understands how important it is to not back down to evil, it would be him. His ability to feel the emotional state of people has given him a unique perspective. Feeling the pain this last push put on our group must have been hard.

"No one should be forced to feel like that again," he urges.

"They're desperate," Caiden adds. "All they have is fear. We already took out their army back there." He points to the forest through which we recently traveled.

"That might be the case," Jax says, "but the deeper we get into this hub, the more we will be exposed to this Influencer."

He looks over to the loyal fighters eagerly awaiting his commands. We sync with him to analyze the group resting against the hub. He shifts his attention back to us. "We've lost four already and it would've been more if Kaylin hadn't broken that push."

"Well, let's see what she has to say, then," Farren says, resting a hand on my back. "She stopped this Influencer once. If anyone has any insight, it would be Kay."

Oh man, this just got real. How can I decide the fate of so many good people? On one hand, this resistance is at a turning point. We'll diminish our chances of winning by sending most of our fighters back. If we don't send them back, though, I become responsible for their mental safety as we press forward as a whole.

"Whoever is doing this can alter the conscious fold faster than me," I say. "I don't know if I can keep pace."

Jax steps in and says, "We can't put this kind of pressure on her. It's too much for anyone."

I enter the center of the leaders' huddle and interrupt Jax. "Hold on a second. I never said we shouldn't do this. I might be scared or even a little unsure, but we will never get this chance again."

"Now you're talking," Caiden blurts out.

"Settle down," says Farren.

If I'm ever going to believe in my ability, now is the time to step up. We have them pinned in a corner. It's time to take them out.

"We need to do this for everyone," I say.

Jax looks at me with those penetrating blue eyes. "I do believe in you and know you're capable of amazing things. I just hope you're sure."

"You know just as well as I do that our reality is shaped by action and intention," I respond. "If we act scared and passive, we'll just be swallowed by Magnus."

Jax agrees, and just like that the leadership has spoken—and I actually had something to say. Now I need to back up my big mouth.

We rejoin the others against the wall. Caiden and Farren move in opposite directions to cover the most ground. They check in with each member to make sure they're ready and focused. From my vantage point near the front of the line, most everyone is ready and still with us. The ones who aren't sure refuse to abandon the rest. They've placed their trust in me and I won't let them down.

A unified rumble trails the leadership as our resistance follows us at an eager pace. We move on toward the east gate that lies just around the wall that we now hug. A cool, gentle breeze flows from around the structure. Loosened strands from my ponytail catch the gust and tickle my sweaty shoulders. Caiden has informed the snipers to rotate around the group. This acts as a moving escort. Our eyes are covering every inch of this structure. With the help of Maddux and the other frontline Influencers, I now cover our minds as well.

Farren takes the lead at the front, followed closely by Jax and Miya. Caiden rejoins us. He's eager for revenge on whoever pushed him to almost kill Tarex. I think it embarrasses him more than angers him. He hates to look weak in front of others.

Not even Jax has been able to connect with the Talas civilians. Their consciousness is there, but something is off. It's like they're sleeping, but their awareness is still moving about inside the hub walls.

While talking to Jax at the Walton hub a couple of days ago, I learned our abilities experience people a little differently. In my mind, I visually see intersecting ripples while Jax senses their presence more. It's like when you know someone is watching you. In this case, it doesn't require people to be looking at him or be anywhere nearby. He can just feel conscious life. The closer the people are, the more intense the feeling is. Then, the more aware they are, the stronger the sense becomes. When two similar sensations happen close together, that's when he knows there's someone he can intimately connect to.

My sole focus now is on that suicide push. I will not let that misery creep into our fighters' minds again. Open and locked in, I become a constant radar for the unshielded. Disconnecting from the current reality makes it hard to stay in the moment while moving. Farren guides me as I rest a hand on his shoulder. Just knowing he's there makes my vulnerable state a little less frightening. Jax follows closely behind as he continues to reach out to the civilians with his push. Being led by Farren and supported by Jax is different. Besides Amanda, no one got more than ten feet from me before we distanced ourselves. It just wasn't smart to get close to anyone with my little secret. It's strange to be part of a family now, if you can even call us that.

Rusted metal doors stand before us. Towering well above, the heavy and impenetrable-looking entrance is our latest obstacle. Beyond this point, Miya informs us there will be several corridors that funnel their ways into different parts of the hub. Her knowledge of this facility rivals even Jax's. She was once very close to the Magnus leadership. The duties she performed allowed for a detailed understanding of where all personnel would be during every type of situation.

When there's a threat to the main entrance, all support staff order the civilians to gather in the inner courtyard for what Magnus calls the Alignment protocol. It's pretty easy to understand what that means. If you keep your herd in one place, then it's easier to prod them into conscious *alignment*. Scattered and afraid, the mind tends to focus on survival. That leads to independent thought, which doesn't fit the sector group's agenda. Civilians are the blood; without them, the whole operation seizes up. With no one there to tend to their lavish needs, these misplaced moguls from the past would live trapped in their isolated castles.

I rest up against the cool, rough structure wall as Farren and Caiden fuse more of Owen's fancy hole-making trinkets to the door. Four or five of them circle the locking mechanism. With a simple swipe on each device, holes are bored through as high-pitched screams escape the dusty smoke from the heated lead panel. Within a few seconds, dull thuds echo from within as the metal fragments drop inside. As expected, a rolling alarm breaches the silence, making it that much harder to concentrate on my task.

Fighters spread out from behind me to flank the door from both sides. Farren asks Caiden to lead, choosing to stay by my side. You won't get any complaints from Caiden about this. If there's a fight to be had, he wants to be front and center.

Two of the bulkier guys dig their fingers into the newly created handholds. Strain floods their faces as they manually pull the doors open. Metal screeches against the concrete foundation. Shifting weapons wave in the air like giant paintbrushes as fighters evaluate the opening. Still there are no signs of resistance.

I catch myself breaking out of the push as my stomach fills with unease. Not long enough to leave us vulnerable, just long enough to stay tuned into the present. Unlike my pushes to shape consciousness, I don't need to close my eyes and completely check out to be effective.

"Playtime," Caiden says to Farren, forcing a grin.

He leads a handful of armed resistance into the opening beyond my viewpoint. Muffled chatter emits from the first of Caiden's team to enter.

"Be vigilant," Maddux whispers to me from behind. His mixed group of fighters and Influencers are the next to move.

"Thanks," I return.

I feel the familiar grip of Farren's long fingers wrap around my wrist. I notice him swallow deeply. Can it be? The fearless Farren Knox is scared? My hand slips down his forearm as I discover a path to intertwine our fingers together. It becomes clear, he's not scared of this fight, but rather he's afraid for me.

"I know I've asked you this before," he says. "Can you please stay with me? I don't want to lose you."

I nod. "I don't really have anything else going on."

I feel his brief chuckle rattle against my shoulder. Contact with him, no matter how short it is, takes my mind off the death and horror that has surrounded me these last few days.

Jax and Miya's groups turn the corner, but are thrust back by an immense, deep boom from inside. Heat rushes from the opening, forcing them to cover their faces with their forearms. A second blast deeper in the hub rattles the hinges of the doors. Farren spins me into his body, shielding me from the heat of the second blast. I peek over his shoulder to see fighters stumble from the opening. One after another they emerge gasping for air and covered in dust. Choking on smoke, Maddux wraps his arm over Caiden's shoulders as they cross the threshold. They stagger to the ground near the metal doors. Miya and a few guys pull them to safety just to the left of the opening.

"They're... gone," stutters Maddux. "They're gone."

"Who is?" Farren insists.

"Nance and Tarex."

Farren steps away from me and approaches Maddux, who sits with his back against the wall. "What do you mean... How?"

"It was Talas civilians strapped with explosives," interrupts Caiden.

Jax kneels beside Caiden. "Did they say anything to you?"

"No, it was like they were zombies. They just strolled up with blank stares."

Not able to believe what I'm hearing, I move to Jax and the others. I replay the last ten minutes in my mind.

"No, no, no," I say. "How can this be? I didn't sense any push. I've been watching for it nonstop."

"You didn't fail," Jax says, shifting his focus from Caiden to me. "Those were Talas civilians."

"Why does that matter?"

"They were molded outside your focus. We were watching out for our own, keeping our unprotected safe. I didn't think about Talas' own civilians."

Drips of disgust trickle into my mind as this sinks in. This heartless Influencer is sending Magnus' own people out as bombs against us. My fists clench at the thought.

"I don't know if I can shield our own while watching the civilians as well," I say.

Farren returns to my side. "We need to find this Influencer before we lose anyone else."

Jax and Caiden agree. Our priorities have to shift from the original plan. No longer is the Magnus Order leadership the main target. Without neutralizing this sick Influencer first, the mission would become far bloodier.

A select group assembles to find and remove this threat before we take this hub. The entire leadership along with a few highly skilled fighters will make their way through this labyrinth of who-knows-what. My ability outweighs everyone's concern for my safety and/or lack of faith in anything else I can bring to the table. I'm the only one who can counter that push. Farren struggles with this decision, but even he knows there is no other way. There's an intensity in his eyes. He's trying to wrestle a new and safer option from his mind. It's time to move and there's no other choice. I have to defuse any other manipulated civilians sent our way.

The clank from my shoes hitting the metal flooring signals the start of the most frightening thing I have ever done. Our army will sit this one out, leaving it up to our specialized collection of teens and young adults. Chills flow down my shoulders to my fingertips as fear swallows me whole. Next up… I have no clue.

25

A FAMILIAR FACE

IT'S A LITTLE unsettling to know our heavily armed fighters have retreated to the safety beyond the outer wall. I know they need to be there so the Influencer can't make them do horrendous things, but it's daunting to be entering the hub with just the leadership and three gunmen. As skilled as we are, it's just nine of us now.

Safely tucked behind the rest, I keep my mind expanded. I watch for any shifts in the current reality. It's dark in these windowless hallways. At least Farren has disabled that distracting alarm. Lifeless and spooky, our surroundings are filled with the unknown.

Some sort of cabling runs across the top of the walls as riveted lines stretch to the cement flooring every five to ten feet. The alarm turned the standard lights off, leaving only a red haze that retracts with each pulse.

Darkness wraps over the hall for a split second between the blips. Miya directs us down a corridor marked B1. According to her, only authorized personnel are ever allowed down any path marked with a B. Jax agrees that if we are going to find this Influencer or the leadership, we need to take the most well-protected route. This makes sense, but just once I would like to take the easier and less dangerous route.

Farren checks in on me, asking if I'm picking up on anything yet. I get the feeling he's checking my state of mind as well. It's hard to respond to him with the setting we're in, but I let him know there's nothing out of the ordinary.

Jax has kept his mind locked on the Talas civilians. Watching innocent humans blow themselves up in front of me would be horrible. If even one of them move from their current state in the inner courtyard, he will know. We're not heading there, but we are close enough for Maddux to get an emotional status of the civilians. He confirms what Jax has been feeling: they're catatonic and almost somehow bored. The hub's Influencers have stripped them of their freewill. We'll deal with them next.

The endless resounding footsteps as we march forward start to blend into a harmonious beat. The tight corridors speed up the echoes that bounce off the walls. My controlled breathing is all that prevents my heart from matching the intense rhythm. We have no chance of catching anyone by surprise, that's for sure. These structures, built to protect the privileged from the world they created, are made to last many lifetimes. Metal and concrete must've been the go-to choice for lair construction when the world blew up.

Led by Miya, we reach the end of the B1 tunnel. Standing in front of us is a metal door with a small window; to the right is a staircase that only heads up. A dull green light hangs from above the first steps. On the wall above the railing, a faded up-arrow next to the designation B2 directs us where to go. She signals us forward and without hesitation, we're on the move up the mesh steps. I peer up to the edge of the green haze only to find endless black. Well, that's just a tad freaky.

We make our turn around the first flight up when a tempered rattling of footsteps fades out in the distance. Farren clutches my untucked shirt, preventing me from moving forward. The group as a whole freezes and becomes silent. We listen for a moment, but hear nothing. Whoever was up there heard us coming and has moved on. From the rear, Caiden squeezes his way to the front. His head tilted, he looks through a small scope on his pistol. Pointing down the pitch-black hallway for a few seconds, he turns to us. "I don't see anyone, but there's a faint glow from the last door down on the right."

He must have a night scope on his gun, because I see zero traces of light besides what remains from behind in the staircase.

"Why is there no light in this hallway?" I whisper to Farren.

He leans down, keeping his sight forward, and replies, "This is standard breach protocol. Keep the intruders in the dark while Magnus waits for their moment to strike."

Just like the rattlesnakes Amanda and I would stumble upon traveling through Lost Souls. They lie in their holes waiting to lunge at your leg if you get too close. Except these snakes have guns, and go for your head instead.

Jax catches the attention of Caiden and then the three gunmen in our group. I don't know their names, but it's best that I avoid small talk. With a few fancy hand gestures, he instructs them to move forward. I can only assume their weapons have night-vision tech as well.

Farren instructs the rest of us to stay several yards back and to not give our position away by using any light sources we might have. It's reassuring to know someone with us at least has a flashlight—even though they can't use it now.

With the three gunmen in front, Caiden reaches the bend at the end of the hallway. He edges from the wall to make sure the next turn is clear before turning back to the source of the light. From where I am, about ten yards back, I now see a faint yellow glow that frames the door.

Farren, with his arm locked across my chest as we tiptoe forward, is not willing to let me move without his permission. Jax and Miya pin me from both sides and

Maddux watches from behind. Boxed in, I have no room to breathe.

"Whoever's in there is shielded," suggests Jax.

Maddux adds from the back, "Yeah, I'm not sensing any emotion or other Influencers either."

"Are you picking up on anything?" Jax asks me.

With all my efforts locked on a certain brand of push, it's not allowing me to expand my ability. I simply reply, "No."

Caiden and the fighters rest against the wall that surrounds the door as they wait for the signal from Jax to move in. With two on each side, they hope to overtake whoever's in there. Anything could be behind this door, and I'm not too excited to find out what. With a simple nod, Jax instructs them to take the room. Caiden gently grabs the lever. Not wanting to pop the hatch too loudly, he pushes down at an anxiety-inducing pace. Despite the effort, the hinges creak and he decides to shove the door wide open. Farren guides the rest of us to back up just outside the door. He and Miya line the wall with their rifles providing cover for the rest of us. Caiden throws his body forward almost as if he wanted that extra force to take on whatever comes. Followed by the fighters, they disappear into the opening. All I can hear is scattered footsteps. It's becoming hard to focus on my main job, but doing this helps me avoid the flood of terror I'm feeling.

Then we hear, "All clear," and the tension breaks.

Farren is the first to move. He slides along the smooth wall before entering. Jax and Miya guide Maddux and me through next. I guess I don't fully trust what I'm told, as I inch my head around the doorframe before entering.

"This is a training room for new personnel," says Miya.

The room is big—like, really big. Several circular lights embedded in the top of the walls illuminate a large open space in the center. The focus of the lamps, trained on the open space, leave the outer parts dim. Other rooms that look like offices extrude from each corner. Each office has glass windows on both the exposed sides. A small workstation and chair are all that are inside. They look like they're used for observation. Turning my attention back to the open space, I see a training floor that has faded blood spattered all over it. There's a familiar musk to the room that reminds me of the cramped shelter dorms. It's not overwhelming, it's just a lingering odor that tickles your nose. A few hanging racks filled with long wooden sticks fill the back wall. Farren tells us this was the Talas dojo. That explains his impressive fighting skills, but it's the last thing we need now—Magnus ninjas jumping out at us.

"No one's in here," says Caiden while he fidgets with the training weapons.

Maddux leans on the wall near the entrance. With his arms folded and his Mohawk now dangling in his eyes due to sweat, he looks impatient. He blows the pitch-black hair from his eyes and says, "Can we stop staring at this blood and move on?"

Just as the words leave his mouth, an arm sneaks from outside the open doorway and clutches his neck. Maddux jolts his head back and slaps at the forearm as he's pulled into the opening. A second arm emerges and jabs a dark object into his throat. A quick electric charge snaps on his neck. Maddux's body tenses. Light from the weapon illuminates the figure behind him. A large man dressed in Magnus apparel towers over Maddux, who stands still as the jolt of electricity sucks the fight from him.

Our group trains our weapons at the entrance. Farren steps in front of me, barely giving me an inch to see. Caiden and the others start yelling at the lurking figure, insisting he release Maddux. The man uses him and the entrance as cover. That's when I hear a familiar voice from the hall say, "Please, now, let's not get barbaric with our discord."

The privileged accent is a dead giveaway. Mavis Edgeley, my former captor from the Hawthorne hub, stretches his tiny, chiseled face over Maddux's shoulder.

"We are going to enter the room now," says Mavis. "I kindly ask you to lower your weapons."

I wonder if that weapon is non-lethal. We could just take that beast down, but we would risk Maddux getting shocked again. But if no one is blasting away, then they probably know more about the tech than I do. Or maybe they don't trust their own aim.

Jax moves to the center of the room with one hand raised. With the other, he lowers his pistol to the ground. After the weapon is resting on the mat, he retreats a few steps and says, "Alright guys, let's do what he asks."

I catch myself drifting from my protective scan of the hub. The safety of Caiden's mind and the thought of more human bombs pull my awareness back. Depressed and armed, Caiden would make this situation much more complicated. I have a lot I want to say to that little man, but I can't focus on him now.

After several disapproving remarks from Caiden, the rest of the group follows Jax's lead and places their weapons next to his.

Still wearing an unnecessary, stuffy suit, Mavis slithers past the man holding Maddux. He and a couple of armed men move from the shadows into the center of the room. They stand several feet from us now. He catches my glance and, with a satisfied smile, says, "Oh, hi, Kaylin, I'm glad we've run into each other."

"You leave her alone," Farren says.

"This is too cute," says Mavis. "Farren Knox has gone from ruthless kidnapper to knight in shining armor."

Farren's anger inches his body forward. This time, I'm the one who holds him back from danger. With his jaw flexed and his brow tensed, I see how much he wants to take down Mavis. I'm able to keep him at bay for now.

Not letting Farren respond, Mavis turns back to Maddux and grabs his dangling bangs, pulling his head up. He leans in and asks, "Where's your better half?"

Maddux's mouth falls open, weakened by the shock. He's awake, but not fully there. I don't think he's able to respond, as he blinks slowly while his eyes wander. The hulking guard is all that's preventing him from buckling to the ground.

Caiden snaps his fingers to grab Mavis's attention and asks, "What do you want with us?"

"Want with you? This has nothing to do with you at all."

He turns back to the group with that cocky smile brimming from his mug. "Your little band of misfits is the last thing on my mind."

I'm done with his little show; I know he loves every minute of it. Not wanting to watch anymore, I blurt out, "Get to the point already."

"Oh, young Kaylin, if it wasn't for this annoying resistance of yours, I would be so ecstatic to once again take you as my prize. But, alas, the days of taking orders from the Magnus Order are numbered. We didn't anticipate Mr. Riley's betrayal."

He pauses for a moment, his eyes trained on Jax. A few seconds pass before he returns his beady gaze to mine. "I'm just passing through now. I don't really care what you do to Magnus. I just came to… settle a score, if you will."

"Settle a score with who?" asks Jax.

"With whom, you ask? Well, I didn't quite enjoy soiling myself and being locked in the darkest parts of my mind for those several hours."

He's talking about the push Ava did on him when we freed Amanda from the Hawthorne hub. We left him paralyzed in fear just inside the hub's outer gate.

"You know what I remember the clearest?" he asks in a raised voice. "I remember watching my sister get murdered and dismembered by filthy Harvesters right in front of my eyes. But what could I do other than stare as she thrashes in pain?"

I see his controlled manner start to crack as he relives the push. His calm demeanor changes to that of a person who truly did lose someone close to them. Knowing how Ava's push works, I suspect Mavis's sister must have truly been killed in some way by Harvesters. Ava's push would have amplified the memory, forcing Mavis to live through the event all over again.

Mavis brushes his fingers through his greasy, slicked-back hair to gather himself, eventually resting his hand on the back of his neck. That smile once again returns and a deep breath resets his uptight default setting. Slowly trotting back to Maddux, he nuzzles his forehead against our friend's and says softly, "She will feel what I felt."

A quick thrust from Mavis's right arm into Maddux's stomach releases a breathless groan. Horrorstruck, I watch as Mavis pulls a darkened blade from Maddux's midsection, spilling blood to the ground.

I can't move. My vision shakes as I nearly pass out. Barely holding myself together, I watch Maddux topple to the floor. A pool of dark blood spreads away from his body. It only takes a few seconds before his eyes shut. Maddux is gone.

26

PERSPECTIVE

SHOUTS OF RAGE blend together as the room teeters at the edge of chaos. The three large rifles pointing at us are the only thing stopping our team from tearing Mavis apart. Jax clings to Caiden's shoulders, nearly ripping his shirt off as he tugs with all his effort to break free. Farren remains still as he shields me from whatever comes next.

"Well, that felt good... Like, real good," says Mavis. "That will hurt her more than anything I could've done to her directly."

Jax has somehow kept Caiden from attacking as the reality of what has happened destroys the spirit of the group. A somber calm takes the place of the anger and we all just retreat to our inner thoughts.

"Now, what to do with the rest of you, hum?" ponders Mavis.

"Let me take care of this, sir," says one of the armed men.

"So many former colleagues and fun new acquaintances all in one place. I've worked with Jax and Miya many times. And then there's my favorite Magnus errand boy, Farren."

The muscles in Farren's arm tighten, but he stays put.

Mavis grabs the shirttail of the nearest guard and wipes Maddux's blood from his hands. The man doesn't even flinch. I suspect horrible treatment is just one more of Mavis's endearing traits.

"We can't forget the all-powerful Kaylin, can we?" asks Mavis. "I would love to offer you all top positions in my next venture, but I suspect that request will not go over too well."

His grin returns. He steps a few feet behind the guards and says, "Tidy this up, gentlemen."

The three gunmen form a clean line and raise their weapons. That's when I feel it. Somehow, the awareness of more people in the room enters my mind. Our captors' implants are disabled and the men are vulnerable. This doesn't make sense, but I don't waste any time questioning it before I shift my focus onto them. My push extends beyond my personal awareness faster than ever before. I encircle their minds with my consciousness. With precision, I flood their reality with feelings of guilt and confusion. The push takes hold and I see glimmers of their thoughts rush at me. I've made them relive Mavis's attack on Maddux. Forced to watch his brutal death again from the guards' perspectives breaks me from the push. Without hesitation, I retrain my attention on any outside push that might take advantage of our exposed team. Still, I have enough concentration to see my push take hold.

"Gentlemen, I don't have all day," says Mavis to his armed escorts.

The three men, locked on us, don't move. The barrels of their guns remain trained on us, but their eyes shift with doubt. Impatient, Mavis grabs the shoulder of the closest man to Farren and me. Rattled into action, the gunman jabs the butt of his weapon into Mavis's chest, sending him back to the wall just near the exit. A pathetic whimper is forced from his throat as he clutches his new injury. "What the hell are you doing?" Mavis demands.

There's a steady increase in unease as uncertainty opens cracks of opportunity for our group. Caiden looks to Farren as if he wants to take advantage of the confusion.

The two other guards remain locked on our team, even as it's clear they're completely wrapped in my push. We just need them to break and we will overtake them.

"It's not alright what you did," says the towering guard as he peers down at Mavis.

"Whoa, whoa, whoa, Ethan," pleads Mavis as he starts to put things together. "Hold on. Don't you see what they're doing? They've somehow disabled your implant and that little brat is controlling you now."

Farren turns to me looking for confirmation of what Mavis is saying. We lock eyes for a moment as he realizes it's true.

The hulking, shaven-headed beast isn't persuaded. He lowers his weapon to his side and, with his other hand, grabs Mavis's tacky velvet tie and uses it as a noose to control his movements. With a simple tug, Ethan pulls Mavis tight into his body as he lowers his thick neck to allow their foreheads to meet. Like a cornered animal, Mavis claws at the man's biceps, hoping to gain an inch of space. The other guards switch between looking over their shoulders at the conflict and re-locking their sights on us.

"That man did not need to die," insists Ethan as he points the barrel of his rifle at Maddux's body. "I'm sick of your little revenge games."

Mavis grunts as Ethan strangles him with his own tie. Desperation prompts the little man to flail his arms in hopes of finding a way free. Shades of deep blue spread across his face without the oxygen his lungs cry for. With little time left, he finds the stun weapon on Ethan's side belt. "Hey, look out," shouts Caiden.

His warning is too late; Ethan stiffens and drops to the ground like a mighty oak. Mavis drops the weapon to loosen the tie that strangles him. The two other guards snap into action and turn on Mavis. This is our chance.

Farren looks to Caiden and I suspect they're thinking the same thing. Without any hesitation, they lunge at the distracted guards. Farren raises his leg and with all his strength hammers down on the closest man's kneecap. The guard's neck flings back as pain forces an inhuman howl from his body. I cringe as he collapses to the ground, then turn to watch Caiden throw an elbow at the other guard's forehead, sending him into an unconscious spin before slamming into Mavis. His limp body pins Mavis to the ground. Farren uses the bottom of his boot to take out the other guard. Mavis is the only one still conscious. His lack of strength prevents him from moving. Watching his pathetic attempts to free himself gives me a small moment of satisfaction between the horrifying and sad events that just took place.

We regain our weapons from the middle of the room before Farren rushes to kneel beside Maddux's body. Caiden searches the gunmen and finds Magnus-issued restraints. While still unconscious, that familiar plastic material molds to the guards' hands and wrists within just a few seconds. One question remains, though, but I didn't have to wait long for the answer. Miya walks up to our huddle and pulls a black and silver device from her long-sleeved top. I recognize it to be one of Owen's block disrupters.

"Those guards weren't very thorough," says Miya. "Wow, this thing really works."

Farren adjusts Maddux's body to a more comfortable-looking resting position. He places him on his back, gently lowering his head to cement still warm from the freshly spilled blood. Even though he knows he is no longer with us, I see this gives Farren a sense of peace. He looks for something to cover his body with, but Jax steps in and says, "We have to keep moving. You know Maddux would tell us not to stop now."

We're interrupted by Mavis as he manages to squirm just enough to sit up against the wall. "Please, I can help you. With my access codes, we can take down this hub. That's what you want, right?"

Caiden's eyes roll back before he turns and stomps over to Mavis. He grabs the stun weapon from the ground. Hands and legs now tied, Mavis slides down the wall as his natural instinct to look out for himself kicks in. Slithering like a snake, he tries to roll away once he realizes what's about to happen. A quick zap seizes his body, putting him out and—thankfully—shutting him up. Caiden hovers over his limp frame for a few seconds, clearly wanting to do more. After a deep exhale, he returns to Maddux.

"Come on, man," Farren says, raising his arms to the ceiling. "How are we supposed to use him like this?"

"We just need his handprint and eyes," says Miya. "He doesn't need to be awake for that."

"I can take care of that right now," Caiden takes out a small blade from his belt.

"Hey, hold on," Jax says, grabbing Caiden's wrist. "That is not who we are. He's coming with us until he becomes useless."

Both Caiden and Farren clearly disagree, but they manage to keep their mouths shut for now. If they had their way, Mavis would be strung up on those racks on the back wall while he slowly bled out. Or maybe that's just my subconscious using them to play out my own desires.

It's settled then: we're taking him to gain access to areas that might cause a problem for us. Refusing to carry him, Caiden leaves that to Jax and a reluctant Farren.

We make a pact to return for Maddux's body once this is over. Ava deserves to see him one last time.

Back in the stale and darkened stairwells, we move up four more levels before Miya and Jax identify the key panel that will lead us into the Magnus executive wing. Windowless, double steel doors stand before us. I'm told that beyond this point is a lavish living area and the control center of the hub. The leadership and their most trusted officers never have to leave this wing to control the entire sector group. It's basically self-sustaining and completely disconnected from the rest of the hub's main systems. Even if a massive radioactive weapon wiped out the entire forest and substructures of the hub, this section would be able to ride it all out in full, lavish style. Hopefully, what lies on the other side of these doors is the resistance's last hurdle to a free and better awareness.

27

INTRODUCTIONS

WE'VE TAKEN OUT the camera that was monitoring us at the entrance. With the surveillance feed cut off, whoever's inside will know that something is up. There will be no way for them to see how many of us there are or our exact location. Miya and Jax believe the executive wing should be mostly undefended. If there were guards left, we would have never made it to this level without a fight. I hope they're right. Let's hope when it's time, Mavis's handprint will access the wing. If not, Caiden will be extremely upset that we brought him with us.

We've dealt with tree-climbing snipers, smoky chaos at the outer gates, evil push attacks, and the painful loss of Maddux to get to this point. This executive wing is all we have left to overcome the Magnus Order's strategic hold on the Southern Coastal region. Once Talas falls, it signals the removal of the corporate head and the rest of the network tumbles into disarray. The civilians will have the chance to regain control. With the pressure of the forced Magnus Influencers lifted, they can choose to stand for the people once again. It won't be easy or clean, but change will come and it will come fast.

Singed rubber from the camera wiring overtakes the musky smell from the hall. Rampant sparks from the torn out device intensify my anxiety. Standing several yards back, Jax, one of our gunmen, and I will wait for the room to be cleared before we move forward. I knew Farren would want to be front and center for this breach, but Caiden, who's beyond fired up, will make them reckless. He wants revenge, and Farren will back him up no matter what.

"Farren, my team will follow you and Caiden in once the room is clear," says Miya. "If they're following protocol, the brothers should be locked in the safe room at the end of the wing. Hopefully, were not too late."

Farren nods, retraining his rifle on the metal door. Miya and the two gunmen in her unit stand behind Caiden and Farren with their rifles butted against their shoulders.

Mavis's limp arm is raised from the wall he's propped against. Caiden positions his hand over the glowing red sensor just left of the door. A green pulse swipes across his palm, which engages a short beep. ACCESS GRANTED flashes atop the display as it brightens the area for a moment. Some sort of internal mechanism triggers a metal thud that comes from inside the door. *Thank God.* I don't know if I could handle Caiden's reaction if that didn't work. Caiden whips Mavis's arm back like a worthless piece of trash. It slams against the wall. Mavis groans, but remains out.

Farren's face flickers into sight as sparks fall down from above before they fade on the ground. He catches Caiden's glance and they signal to each other. With Jax constantly in front of me, I find it hard to maintain this vantage point. That, combined with the darkness of this corridor, leaves my mind to imagine more than it should.

"Alright, let's move," Farren says as he and Caiden lean on the heavy doors.

A thunder-like sound rolls from the entrance as it gains momentum. With one hand resting on Jax' shoulder, I pull myself up to my tiptoes. The others raise their weapons and crouch through the opening. With the door breached, Miya and her team move next.

Cracks blare from inside the room just after Farren makes it through. I realize then that Magnus guards were just waiting for us to open that door. Forced back by the barrage of shots, one of our gunmen slams into Miya as his body collapses. Pinned down, she cries out in pain. Bullets continue to slam against the wall across from the entrance, rapid like a heavy hailstorm pelting a metal roof. A deeper moan filters through the madness. The wounded fighter from Miya's group retreats just outside the door next to Mavis's unconscious body. Unable to sit still, he clutches his calf with both hands. The bullets won't stop. *Farren is all I can think of now. Are they pinned down? Why have they not pulled back into the corridor?* Jax slams into my chest and forces me back.

"No, we can't leave without them," I yell.

The resistance fighter who was held back nods at Jax as he rushes to the entrance to give whatever support he can. The endless bullets send him to the wall just outside the room. The dust and paint flecked from the bullet holes filters back to us, making my eyes water. I can't take much more of this. *Please stop firing.*

A dark figure emerges from outside the entrance. I squint, but it doesn't help. The battle is kicking everything up into this narrow space. The blasts continue to pulsate in my ears. Covering them muffles the constant buzz a bit, but not enough. I recognize the person just beyond the haze. It's Mavis. He's confused and teetering from side to side. The full effects of the shock weapon haven't worn off. He stumbles into the opening. Ripping through every inch of him, bullets exit his body as blood splatters against the wall. His shoulder dips back while his knees buckle. Each new blast distorts his gradual fall to the ground. A crippled pile is all that remains of Mavis Edgeley.

An explosion booms as the shockwave vibrates past our feet. Heat rushes from the opening. I collapse and cover my head. Jax tackles me and shields me from the exhaust. The cool air returns and we notice the bullets have stopped. I nearly push Jax off of me while rushing to the entrance. My arm is snapped back as Jax grabs my wrist. "Please, I have to find him."

"Just wait a second, Kaylin," he insists.

With his free hand, he pulls out his pistol and holds it to his side. Moving in front of me, he releases my arm, but keeps his hand raised to prevent me from darting forward. He leans in and spots movement from a pile of bodies ahead. Miya wrestles her arm free from the charred resistance fighter that toppled on top of her. His body saved her from the explosion. Jax grabs her arm, keeping his gun pointed into the smoke-blurred entrance. He pulls her a few feet into the hallway. She coughs several times, which loosens the soot from her matted hair. Pops from the exposed wires continue to give temporary bursts of light. Kneeling beside her, I rip a piece of my shirt. Placing the cloth on a small, bloody wound on the back of her head, I'm able to control the bleeding. She winces before gathering herself. Turning, I find Jax has moved on to the support gunmen in our group. It doesn't take long to realize both of them were killed by the blast. Burned and unrecognizable, the men had no chance to avoid the extreme energy of the explosion. My breath stutters as I inhale. Three more lives lost. Our group, nearly cut in half now, is broken, scattered, and lost. I'm afraid to think of Farren and Caiden, not ready to add them to the list.

"Kaylin… Jax," is shouted from inside.

"Farren!" I respond, stumbling through the devastation.

Yet again Jax restrains me before I blindly run into the murky unknown. His arm stretches across my shoulders, dragging me to the side just past one of the fallen men, his weapon drawn as his back slams against the wall. The smoke cloud that entrapped the opening flushes into disarray as Farren races through. He's alive. Jax releases me and I jump into Farren's arms, not giving him a moment to search for me. He stumbles back a bit before he realizes it's me.

He returns a tight embrace and asks, "Are you alright?"

"Yes, are you?"

Exchanging smiles, we look each other over for wounds. His grit-filled hands clasp my cheeks, pulling me up to meet our foreheads. "I'm fine."

Coughing, Caiden emerges from the thinning smoke to witness the losses to our team. He wasn't close to them, but his military mindset leads to a deep bond with fellow soldiers. It doesn't take long before his somber mood changes to satisfaction as he notices Mavis's nearly unrecognizable body lying at his feet. Even with the burns and bullet holes, that smug face shines through as if he's giving us one last jab from the grave.

Miya joins our decimated group as we reconnect in the hall. The bleeding at the back of her head has stopped and she's regained her strength. Trying to figure it out, I ask Farren, "What happened in there?"

"There were five or six heavily armed Magnus fighters concealed all throughout the first room," Farren explains, giving Miya a puzzled look.

Her intel was wrong—she of all people should have known every possible scenario when it came to the Magnus Order's leadership.

Caiden interrupts him. "Well, it doesn't matter anyway, the safe room was empty."

"I don't understand, Percy and Harold have to be here," Miya says, rubbing the back of her head.

"They were here when I left," Jax says. "And no place in the Magnus sector is safer than Talas. They rarely leave this place."

"What was that explosion?" Jax asks.

"Oh, that little thing," Caiden says, wiping the soot from his face. "Well, I peppered one of the snipers in the back and as she fell, her gun kept blasting away. She tagged a few propane tanks in the back. If it wasn't for that concrete wall, we'd be dust right now."

"So what were they protecting if the safe room was empty?" Miya asks.

Farren shifts his focus back to the entrance. "Those guards were protecting a staircase near the back."

"The helipad," insists Miya. "Let's move."

"Are you sure?" Jax asks, examining her wounds. "We can lead you back to the others before we move on."

"It will be too late by then, and I'm not missing this. I'm fine."

A quick check on ammo and the team is ready. Jax and I scan the area for anything abnormal, including our evil Influencer friend. No gloomy pushes, no signs of incoming civilians—nothing.

Led by Farren, we enter the executive wing. The dust and smoke have settled, but the smell of charred bodies is intense. Miya almost loses it at the stench. Her shirt collar is enough to get her through it.

This operations room is big and, even with that explosion knocking out everything, some lights in the high ceilings remain functional. It reminds me of a shelter mess hall: expansive and cold. The lack of color or comfort is obvious. This room is all about function over style. Melted comm stations sit below a wall of glass monitors that stretch across one of the far corners. Darkened by the blasts, this tech that connects the Talas hub to the rest of the Magnus network is now severed.

I stiffen my neck and keep my eyes forward to avoid the disfigured remains that litter the floor. I've seen enough death for one day—for a lifetime, actually. We pick up the pace to the stairs, passing several hallways that lead deeper into this wing. Every corner of this place has been cleared by our team. Farren and Caiden are the first to the bottom of the spiral metal staircase. Their weapons point up and we remain focused. We want to avoid another ambush. Miya pushes her way to the front. She's eager to once again come face to face with the

Magnus brothers. That taste of doing their dirty work must be tough to forget. Or maybe she just wants to be out of this deathtrap once and for all. I don't blame her.

Our steps echo as we file to the top. I'm the second-to-last to reach the end of the stairwell. A short ladder at the edge of the landing leads up to a large square hatch. This will take us to the roof level. Jax grabs Miya's arm, preventing her from climbing up. "Hey, just wait a second," he insists.

"They have to be up there. We need to move," she says, shrugging her arm free.

Farren notices her irrational behavior and steps in front of her. "I understand this has been a long time coming for you, but blindly popping your head out a gopher hole is not your best move."

She takes a deep breath and exhales slowly, which seems to settle her. "Okay, so what's our move?"

Farren defers to Caiden for the safest approach. Scratching his overgrown red sideburns, Caiden tries to stir up ideas. "There's no pretty way to do this. I'll open while the rest of you keep your weapons trained on whatever fun comes next."

"We don't really have a lot of choices here," I say.

Without another word said, we all adjust our positions and prepare for whatever is on the other side of this hatch. Farren guides me a few steps down and hands me a small pistol. "This is a G-Pulse firearm. It's simple to use, light, and deadly."

His eyes have an unfamiliar intensity as they burn into mine. He gives me a quick lesson on how to fire the weapon. He's all business right now. He's scared for me; I don't need to be in his mind to know that. With my free arm, I caress his forearm, petting it with my thumb. I smirk and say, "Don't worry, I had twenty minutes of weapons training at the Walton hub."

I'm unable to get a smile from him this time. I can't overthink this now. We're about to crack this lid. Moving a few steps down, our group fans out around Caiden with guns locked on the hatch. Caiden silently counts down on his raised fingers.

Three…

Two…

One.

The latch is forced open as light floods in, blinding us for a moment before our eyes adjust. To our surprise, there's nothing. No explosion, no gunfire, nothing.

Jax waves his hand up and down in a calming motion as he moves to the front. He sneaks a glance through the opening before turning to Farren and Caiden. With a nod, he signals them to move up the ladder. Miya grabs Farren's shoulder just before he reaches the bottom rung and nods toward me. "Stay with her and keep her secure. I've got this."

She's still eager to be front and center. Miya is always following procedures, so this impulse for revenge is out of place. I do feel comfortable with Farren by my side, though, but I'm nervous for her as well. Farren agrees with her as he falls back to my side just off the landing.

Gripping her weapon in one hand, she uses the other to climb the short ladder. Caiden is practically bouncing in place behind her. She's up and out of sight now. Jax keeps Caiden from flying up until we hear the all-clear. The wait isn't very long as her faded voice lets us know we're good to move.

One by one, we breach the crisp air and find ourselves standing in the open space on the top of this hub. We fan out, circling a red marked symbol painted beneath our feet. "It's the helipad for their FlexViper," Miya says to me.

"They're gone, we're too late," Caiden says, flailing his arms to the sky. His disappointment pours out and anger takes over.

Farren turns to Miya. "Did you clear the whole roof?"

Other than a few antenna arrays, floodlights, and solar panels, there is not much up here.

"Of course I did."

"Wait, what does this mean for the mission?" I ask, though I already have a pretty good idea.

"The Magnus brothers will just set up headquarters at one of the other hubs," says Miya. "They will rebound from this as long as those two are alive."

Our group's emotions are starting to escape as the unfinished ending is starting is sink in. Caiden moves to the outer wall and dangles his feet off the edge as his head drops low in an almost- comical pout. As poised as ever, Jax is reevaluating the mission, looking for new solutions as he paces back and forth. Disappointment hasn't eluded Farren either, hunched over the opposite wall, scouring the hub's surroundings as he lets off steam. Miya has stormed off toward the far side of the roof. For me, I remain in the center of the helipad hoping for a new outcome to magically appear.

I decide sitting is a better use of my time than pacing or pouting. My hands support my head as I let my mind remember Maddux. I only knew him for a few days, but his warmth and spirit gained a special place in my heart. Awareness is about emotions and connections, not about the length of time. My thoughts move from Maddux to Ava. A tear runs down my cheek and splashes on my forearm. Playing with the cool trails of moisture that stream down my arm, I search for connected emotion that is tangible. Breaking me from my state, a shadow crosses over my legs. I don't even have a second to lift my head before an unfamiliar voice in the distance says, "Hello, everyone."

Scuttling back along the rough ground, I gather my balance before pulling myself up. Turning to the voice, I see two older men walking toward us with their hands raised. They must be the Magnus brothers. Next to them, another man holds a gun to Miya's head. She's still and her face is pale. Several rushed footsteps scuffle behind me. The taller of the older men steps forward, keeping his hands out to show he is unarmed. He surveys our group and in a deep voice says, "I must say, I've never seen a more well-organized bunch of kids. Most of these silly resistances are more like children running away from home—soon they realize there's just no point and they crawl back."

"You need to let her go, Harold," Jax says.

"Oh, Mr. Riley, you have disappointed me. We've given you so much, and this is how you repay our generosity."

His well-groomed, whitened beard and weathered face stir up a primal sense of respect, although my mind knows better. Their tailored suits reignite that raw emotion Mavis stirred up. They walk differently too, like the fancy clothes straighten them up and force them to puff out their chests. It's disgusting. If he's Harold, the other one crossing his arms must be Percy.

"It's okay, Harold," says Percy. "Mr. Riley's services are no longer needed. Not now that we have Mr. Stratton here."

My breathing quickens at the realization that the guy restraining Miya must be the evil Influencer. Glancing over, I find his dark eyes trained on me. I thought he was just Magnus personnel but, like most Influencers, he is young. If it wasn't for the emotional weight lying behind his eyes, he could be younger than me. His black hair matches the dark outfit he wears. The high, chunky boots and well-fitted button-up shirt look like something Caiden would wear.

"Why don't you lower your weapon and we'll do the same," pleads Jax.

"That's just silly," Harold says, grinning at Percy. "If we drop our weapon, you could overtake us with your numbers."

"You're damn right," says Caiden.

Jax turns to Caiden, lips pursed in frustration. He doesn't need anyone else escalating things.

Harold retrains his green eyes on Jax. "This is what's going to happen. When our FlexViper arrives, Ms. Hurley will come along for a quick ride. Once we are clear, you have my word we will let her go."

Almost as if on cue, a soft wind-driven hum emerges in the distance. The hum becomes a loud whoosh as the craft approaches the hub. It's above us within seconds, forcing us to step to the outer edges of the pad. Our group tightens its formation. We shield our eyes from the dust kicked up from the two lift blades. This FlexViper is fancier than anything I have ever seen. Its smooth edges and black, shiny body gives it the look of speed. Squinting to avoid debris, I notice that there is no one in the cockpit. The brothers must have activated the fully automated craft to approach Talas. The wind weakens as the engines shut down. The blades stop as it becomes silent. There's a pop on each side as doors rise open, giving the look of wings.

"Well, it's time to clean up the mess you've made," Percy says to us as he approaches the opening on the opposite side from where we stand.

"I take your silence as acceptance of our terms," suggests Harold.

Agitated, Farren is having a hard time standing still. I can see in his face that he wants to do something. Jax stands in front of our team, his arms outstretched, keeping us from charging.

"This is not over," Jax says to the brothers.

"You might've shut down Talas, but the Order will remain strong," says Harold as he climbs into the cockpit next to Percy.

Pushed to the craft by Stratton, Miya avoids eye contact with our group. My stomach seizes as I feel for her. A few feet before the Viper, Stratton stops and looks at the brothers.

"What's the holdup?" asks Percy.

"There's going to be a slight change of plans," says Stratton as he pulls Miya's Block Disrupter from his side. He points the device at the brothers. They recognize what he has and grasp at their safety belts trying to get loose to take cover. The device pulses a wave out that passes through the brothers in their seats. He turns to me with the slight shake of his head and taps his pistol at Miya's temple. He knows I would counter his push if it wasn't for Miya's safety. Like the rest of us, the events have locked me in confusion. We have no choice but to watch this play out.

28

LEVERAGE

CONFUSION ENTERS THE rooftop and I ask, "What are you doing?"

"Give me a minute," Stratton says to me as he turns to the brothers. "I have some loose ends to take care of."

With his arm wedged under Miya's armpit, he locks her up as the barrel of his weapon drives her head against his neck. With his right arm, he stuffs the disrupter into his pocket. Jax is having a hard time holding Caiden and Farren back. They're in constant movement, fidgeting and eager to attack. I turn to Farren and put my free hand on his chest. Looking up, I remind him that we'll only get Miya killed if we act now.

Harold and Percy sit still in the FlexViper. They know the device has made them vulnerable to a push. "What are you up to, Stratton?" Harold demands.

Dismissing the brother, he turns to Jax. "I understand why you couldn't stand working for these archaic, self-absorbed fools."

Stratton drags Miya with him as he approaches the brothers. He undoes the top button on his shirt and stretches his neck. "Now, that feels better. Why you force your people to wear this crap is beyond me. Your corporate ways have been obsolete for decades. Your time—"

Percy waves his arms, interrupting him. "Enough. What the hell is this?"

"Your part has played out. I'm done with you," says Stratton.

His eyes close and I know what that means. Without hesitation, I shield Caiden from whatever might come next. He and Farren keep their weapons trained on Stratton, waiting for an opportunity. Nothing leaks into Caiden's awareness. The push is not including him.

Percy's breathing becomes labored. He clamps down on Harold's shoulder, looking for help. Panic pours over his face. Harold's attention becomes scattered. He too is unable to maintain his composure. Turning to Percy, Harold guides the younger brother out of the craft. Both of them are fully engaged in the push. Disconnected from the moment, their altered reality is playing out in front of us all.

Maybe it's because I personally don't know the Magnus brothers, but I find myself fearing for them. We are all conscious and connected, no matter how screwed up we can become as individuals.

The brothers embrace as they walk from the FlexViper toward the outer wall on the opposite side of us. Tears stream from their eyes as some sort of emotional havoc has infected their minds. Stratton's ability is so precise and effective. Even Caiden has stopped pacing in place to watch.

"It doesn't have to end like this," I say. "No one deserves whatever you are going to do."

"I could've shot them if I wanted to be boring," says Stratton. "You of all people should understand that our abilities make us gods to them."

It doesn't matter what I say, the push has taken full effect as the brothers walk straight up to the edge of the thigh-high wall. Without losing stride, they step over. Farren grabs my waist as my instincts draw me to run to help. There's nothing I can do, they have fallen ten stories to the outer courtyard. They didn't even scream; they were completely committed to dying.

Jax steps a few feet from our group and asks, "What is the point of all this? Are you trying to take over Magnus?"

"We don't want to take this group over. We've propped up your resistance from the very beginning to help us tear them down."

"What do you mean, you propped us up?" asks Farren.

"Well, not me exactly, but *us*. The Vernon Society."

Caiden explodes in laughter, nearly dropping to his knees. "That's the stupidest thing I've ever heard."

Stratton stiffens at the reaction. He points his weapon at Caiden only to have his arm slowly lowered by Miya. With ease and no resistance, she removes herself from his grip. She slides in front of him almost as if she's shielding him from us. The panic is gone from her face. In its place is a determined confidence.

Farren shifts his weapon in her direction as he tries to find an angle around her. Confused, he asks, "What's going on? What are you doing to her?"

"He is not doing anything to me," Miya volunteers. "I work with them, too."

My mind disconnects from protecting Caiden as I wonder what is going on. Miya works with them? This is not making any sense. She is our friend and has been working with Farren for years.

"Hold on, hold on." Farren grabs the back of his neck, trying to wrap his head around what he's hearing. "What do you mean? Are you saying you work with the Vernon Society?"

"I'm sorry you were left in the dark," says Miya. "The idea of working for another sector group wouldn't fly with you."

The Vernon Society is the same sector group that attacked the Magnus convoy that was originally transferring me to Talas. Was that all part of some sick plan to use me to help bring down Magnus? None of this feels real to me.

Caiden bumps into Farren as he steps to the front of the craft and asks, "What's stopping us from just ending this and putting a couple of holes in your heads?"

Not wanting to get peppered by bullets, Stratton holds his hand up and then slowly reaches into his front shirt pocket. Carefully drawn out inch by inch, a strand of gold that connects to a familiar-looking pendant falls out. I reach for my necklace, thinking I've somehow lost it, but find it tucked under the collar of my shirt as usual. I don't understand how he could have the same one.

"Where did you get that?" I demand.

"Oh, this little thing," Stratton says, gleeful pride overtaking his face.

"That's enough, Stratton," Miya says before turning back to me. "The Society doesn't just want to take down Magnus. We have bigger plans, and they involve you, Kaylin."

A subtle laugh slips out and Stratton looks at me. "It's not about Magnus, Kaylin. It's about you… Oh, and your brother, too." He points directly at Jax.

What is he talking about? Jax and I turn to each other, desperate for answers.

"Her brother?" Jax's brow tightens.

"Oh, come on," Stratton says, wrapping the necklace around his neck. "You guys really had no idea you're brother and sister?"

Farren moves to the front, forcing Stratton to retrain his weapon on the group. "Why should we believe any of this?"

"Do you see this pretty little trinket?" Stratton points to the pendant. "It's insurance. I'm not sure why, but as soon as you stumbled upon Kaylin, everything became about bringing Jax and her together. For some reason, the Society thinks they're special."

"Wait..." I pause. "Whose necklace is that and why do you have it?"

Miya inches closer to me and says, "It's your mother's, Kaylin."

The word 'mother' blares out at me. I don't have a mother... I don't have a family... I only have Amanda. I shouldn't feel this way, but Miya saying this jabs right at my gut. I've been without a family for so long that what they are saying makes no sense to me.

"Wait, are you saying my parents are still alive?" asks Jax.

He joined Magnus with the one goal of taking down the Society in order to reunite with them. Starting our resistance against the Magnus Order was his way of letting them go after so many years.

"Oh, they're fine as long as you both join us for a little Viper ride," says Stratton.

"Wait a minute," demands Farren. "They're not going anywhere with you."

Jax rests an understanding hand on Farren's shoulder and says, "Hold on, Farren, let me figure this out."

Farren places his hands at his sides before looking to me. He understands what Stratton is demanding of me and it's stirring his emotions.

I holster my weapon and with a deep breath gather myself. Slowly I walk toward Stratton. He raises his weapon before Miya eases his arm down again. She can see I'm not a threat at the moment.

"Kaylin, stop!" shouts Farren.

"Please wait," I urge.

With each step, my stomach churns more, but curiosity drives me forward. "I want to see it," I insist.

Stratton looks to Miya as I stand just a few feet from them now. She nods and he removes the necklace from his sweaty neck and hands it to me.

The gold necklace is tarnished. It barely holds the glimmer of the afternoon sun. I press my fingers along the delicate interlocked chains and follow it down to the pendant. Dinged and scuffed, it has seen better days. But it is exactly the same as mine. Only a few people have ever seen the one I conceal beneath my shirt. Miya is not one of them. You don't find jewelry makers anymore. Especially anyone who can do the intricate work it took to craft these pieces.

"How did you get it from her?"

"She gave it to us," says Miya.

Stratton rips the necklace from my hand and adds, "Your mother understands that we either bring you two into the family or the Society will prevent anyone else from using your gifts. It's that simple."

Silence falls over the group. A few seconds pass before Jax asks, "What about my father? Is he safe?"

"They are together and comfortable," says Miya as she avoids Jax's eyes. "I know they're important to you. You'll see them again if you come with us."

Stratton adds, "But this doesn't work unless you both come, you understand?"

Shifting my attention back and forth between them and our group, I turn to Miya and say, "Give us a minute, will you?"

I get an impatient huff from Stratton and an understanding nod from Miya before I slowly walk back to join the others. Miya was so convincing as part of our resistance. She really did fool us all. How she could work so closely with Farren and Jax only to turn on them is shocking.

Caiden is not thrilled with what he's hearing. The idea that we have all been played for the benefit of another sector group forces him into an unyielding, folded-arms stance. The tightened brows and frozen scowl make it certain. He is furious.

Farren leans up against the perimeter wall unable to stand anymore with the uncertainty weighing him down. Shoulders slumped and legs crossed, he knows this doesn't end well no matter what we do. All I can offer is a supportive smile and a gentle touch to his hand before I turn to Jax.

Jax is scanning me with an intensity I haven't seen from him before. His expression changes from his normal peaceful demeanor into a frantic glare. "I knew I had a sister when I was very young, but she died."

I rest a hand on his forearm, trying to settle his uncertainty. This only amplifies his state. The way he carries himself now reminds me of myself. How I never recognized this before is crazy. There was something there from the first time we met. An inner caring for someone you just met didn't make sense, but it does now.

"Why would my parents lie to me about you? Why were you separated from us?"

I know his questions are not something I can answer, but he is processing this and I want to be there for him. I lean in and say, "I'm sorry. I know this is hard to accept."

"Just because of some necklace, we're going to buy this crap?" Caiden says as he again paces back and forth.

"It all makes sense. Everything is lining up," insists Jax. "If Kaylin is my sister and my parents are alive, I have to know. I just have to."

Farren takes my arm and pulls me a few feet from the group. Stratton adjusts to keep a better eye on us. I can tell he doesn't like our little huddle over here.

"You can't do this," Farren insists. "Just because he has the same necklace doesn't mean he's telling the truth about any of this. They're not going to let me come with you. I can't keep you safe."

"I understand, but there's no way they could know about my necklace. And the way I felt bonded to Jax from the first time we met makes it feel real. I need to find out why I was left behind." I inch closer to him. "It won't be the last time I see you, I promise."

Farren is silent for a moment before he places the cool metal of his weapon on the small of my back, pulling me closer to his warm core. His soft fingertips slide across my temple as he brushes a few loosened strands of my ponytail from my eyes. Following the lines of my cheekbones, he tilts my chin up as he makes eye contact. The deepness of his gaze gives me confidence in what he says next. "I will find you."

Our lips meet for a brief moment. I'm not ready to let go, so I tug on the back of his shirt hoping to somehow absorb him into my consciousness and take him with me. One last kiss on my forehead reminds me of the delicate nature of what we have started. He releases me, not knowing what will happen once I leave this rooftop.

Caiden wraps an arm around his neck, pulling Farren back a step, and jokes, "Don't worry, I will keep him warm at night."

His humor helps me hold back the emotions that have seeped to the surface. I return a smile before looking to Jax. He nods at Caiden and Farren before leading us to the FlexViper. He reaches back for my hand and with hope I take it. In this moment, I have a brother, as well as a mother and father waiting for me at the Vernon Society.

Leaving people behind has never felt so heavy before. Not allowing myself to make new connections has always shielded me, but this time is different. Amanda has the resistance to look after her now. I wish I could say goodbye, but she will be safe and I WILL see her again. Something that I'm leaving unfinished is dominating my thoughts now. It's a new feeling that claws at my heart. It's the confusion and uncertainty that surrounds Farren and me. Even with my limited experience, I can only find one word to describe it.

Love.

End of Book One

***

Thank you for reading book one of the Influence series. If you enjoyed reading this book, please remember to leave a review on Amazon. Positive reviews are the best way to thank an author for writing a book you loved. When a book has a lot of reviews, Amazon will show that book to more potential readers. The review does not have to be long—one or two sentences are just fine! I read all my reviews and appreciate each one of them!

Free Content and Updates on Book 2: Be the first to find out when book two of the Influence series will release. Also, get exclusive content, short stories, giveaway opportunities, and other exclusive bonuses by joining my VIP List.

Join The Resistance:

www.davidrbernstein.com

Acknowledgements:

Special thanks to my wife for her support on this journey!

Thank you to my Mother-in-law for being an early reader and giving great feedback.

Thanks to all my family for the support!

Credits:

Jen Blood - Editor

Patti Geesey - Editor

AAYAA - Publishing and Marketing Support

Leia Stone - Positive Motivation and Publishing Support

Made in the USA
Lexington, KY
09 November 2016